SUMMER UNDER THE *Stars*

SUMMER UNDER THE

KATE MALLINDER

First published in 2025
by Firefly Press
Britannia House, Van Road, Caerphilly CF83 3GG
www.fireflypress.co.uk

© Kate Mallinder 2025

The author asserts her moral right to be identified as author in accordance with the Copyright, Designs and Patent Act, 1988.

All rights reserved.
This book is sold subject to the condition that it shall not, by way of trade or otherwise, be lent, re-sold, hired out or otherwise circulated without the publisher's prior consent in any form, binding or cover other than that in which it is published and without a similar condition including this condition being imposed on the subsequent purchaser.

All characters in this publication are fictitious and any resemblance to real persons, living or dead, is purely coincidental.

A CIP catalogue record of this book is available from the British Library.

ISBN 978-1-913102-85-2

This book has been published with the support of the Welsh Books Council.

Typeset by Elaine Sharples

Printed and bound by
CPI Group (UK) Ltd, Croydon, Surrey, CR0 4YY

To Zoe Cookson, without whose friendship and encouragement this story would never have existed.

CHAPTER 1
SASHA

Thursday evening

My phone flashes. I'm lying on my bed, holding it in front of me, feeling it pulse. She's ringing again. It's Clarisse – my dad's fiancée – and it's the third time in half an hour. There's no point in answering as I already know what she wants. There's no way I'm changing my mind and I'll one hundred per cent upset her by telling her so.

She rings off and seconds later she sends a text. I tap to read, no harm in that.

Sasha. Please. I just want to talk. I know you're upset, and I understand why. Ring me, okay?

I suppose if I spoke to her at least she might stop ringing. Almost certainly if I tell her what I'm thinking.

She answers on the second ring. 'Sasha! *Ma belle*. Thank you.'

'No worries,' I say, propping myself up with my pillow. 'What do you want?'

I must have caught her off-guard with my directness. I hear her take a deep breath.

'Your father's very upset.'

This isn't news. He's been 'upset' and 'disappointed' with me for several weeks now.

'I know he said some stuff he shouldn't have.'

She's got that right.

'And maybe you did too.'

I tense. I never quite know where Clarisse stands. Is she a friend or a foe? Team Dad or Team Sasha?

'It's just, it's our wedding. And I know your father … well, it would mean the world to him if you were there.'

'Why can't he ring and tell me that?'

'You know him. He's a very stubborn man.'

I'm glad she knows, to be honest. To marry him and then find it out would be a real kicker.

'Does he know you're ringing me?'

She pauses. That answers that question.

'Look, Clarisse. Dad said some really hurtful crap. If he's actually sorry, he knows where I am.

And if he really wants me at his wedding, he can tell me that too. He's a grown-up. He shouldn't expect you to go around apologising for him.'

She mutters something under her breath in French. Could swear she said I'm as stubborn as Dad.

'Is there nothing I can say to persuade you? You're supposed to be my bridesmaid. I was so looking forward to becoming part of your family.'

Yeah, who wouldn't want to be part of this dysfunction? 'Sorry, Clarisse. I'm not coming.'

She's quiet for a moment. 'Of course. I totally respect your decision. But know that you will be missed. By me and by your dad.' She hangs up.

I lie on my bed and stare up at the ceiling. Mum isn't home yet so there's no one to distract me from my thoughts. I hadn't meant for this to happen. It sort of just did. First, I'd got the wrong weekend for the dress fitting. And then, when I did get there, I'd been 'too honest' about the dress. For the record, it was *the* most awful bridesmaid dress I'd ever seen. Zero exaggeration. It was hideous. Think wrong length, wrong colour, wrong fabric, wrong style. Were all the bridesmaids going to wear this? If Clarisse was going for the meringue look, then she'd missed it and got blancmange.

At least I hadn't said *that*.

All I'd said was that it was *interesting*. Clarisse started saying maybe it could be switched for a different style, but Dad jumped in and took issue with my 'attitude'. He had a good old rant about me being unreliable, which was a bit rich coming from the man who said goodbye one morning, left for France, and didn't see me for five months. Hardly a beacon of reliability.

He said he wanted to give Clarisse a fairy-tale wedding – the works: a sprawling country house on the clifftops of Marseille and the best caterers in France. He's fixated on it being a Cinderella day.

I said that judging by this dress I was all set to be the ugly step-daughter.

That didn't go down too well.

At all.

He went on about everything he'd done for me and how all he wanted was one day. One day that went smoothly without me ruining it.

And that was it. I wasn't going to ruin it for him. I wouldn't be there. Just one less bridesmaid. No possibility of me ruining anything that way.

I cancelled the flights, told Mum I wouldn't be going and put the whole thing out of my head. Or at least I was trying to. But Dad's words kept going round and round in my mind, playing over and over, churning and churning.

I take a deep breath. I'm not going to let him get to me. I'm not.

'Sasha? Are you in?' It's Mum, home from work.

I crawl off my bed and go downstairs, two at a time.

'Grab the other bag off the doorstep, will you?' Mum's carrying the shopping through to the kitchen. 'How was your day?'

I bring the shopping in and push the front door shut. 'I survived. At least it's nearly the holidays.'

'I used to love the summer holidays. Just days and days stretching in front of you and not a care in the world.'

I smile. Mum suffers from a serious case of rose-tinted spectacles.

'Have you and the girls got everything planned for your trip?'

'Pretty much,' I say as I put cucumber and tomatoes into the fridge. 'Though if you want specifics, you'll have to ask Hetal. She's the one organising everything.'

We've got nearly a week of camping in the Lake District in twelve days' time. I have an app that's counting down the minutes. It was Hetal who pointed out that this might be our last chance to have a trip all together: me, Hetal, Cam and Nell. This time next year Hetal will be off to uni – the one she has her heart set on has a summer introduction course – and I'll be off travelling the instant my exams are done. So, this is our summer. And I can't wait to spend some time with them: no one having to rush off, no one having to leave to work a shift or revise or anything. It's been seriously ages since we've all been together. It'll be just us for a whole week. And I can't wait to chill, chat and catch up with everyone.

'It isn't too long until the wedding either, is it?' Mum's not looking at me, but I can hear her thoughts as loudly as if she's shouting them.

'It's ten days. And I'm not going.'

She holds her hands up. 'And that's fine by me. Whatever you decide, I support your choice.'

Mum always does this. Says she supports my decisions when I know she doesn't. She never *says* anything; I can just tell. She's so obvious.

'Thanks, Mum. That means a lot.' I flick the kettle on for Mum's tea addiction.

'It's just…'

'Just what, Mum?'

'It's your dad. He's getting married. Don't you want to be there?'

'Why do you even care about him, Mum?'

She comes over to me and puts her arm around me. 'I care about you. I don't know what's gone on between you,' – she holds up her hands again – 'and I don't want to. But don't throw everything away over something unimportant.'

'Don't worry about it, Mum. I'm absolutely fine with my decision.'

My relationship with my dad isn't 'everything' and I'm not throwing it away over 'nothing'.

CHAPTER 2
HETAL

Friday

I'm five minutes early for my next class so I take the time to review my day's to-do list. Feels like holidays take as much organising as homework and revision. More possibly.

- Go over the list of camping equipment we need and check everyone's got what they said they would bring (most essential, Nell – a four-berth tent; Cam – camping stove; Sasha – inflatable sofa)
- Double-check our campsite booking
- Research nearby walks/sights/cafés/supermarkets
- Find some ideas for easy camp food
- Download a spooky ghost story

- Pick up Gran's birthday cake
- Call Finn.

Holidays may be lots of organising, but they're So Much Better than schoolwork and our Lake District trip is going to be the best holiday of all time. We'd promised last year to be friends forever, but that feels a bit forgotten at the moment. But this trip. This trip is going to bring us back together again.

The bell goes and I follow everyone crowding in through the door to chemistry. It's a bright room with windows all along one wall and wooden benches in rows. I go and sit in my usual spot, halfway back next to Rosie. She grins at me as I slide into my seat. Everyone else in my class looks like I feel – exhausted but excited that the term is nearly done.

'Okay, everyone, settle down,' says Mr Nolan from the front. He's your cliché science teacher: white coat, mad hair. Einstein's clearly his style icon. 'Today we're going through your exam papers from last week.'

There's a collective groan. I miss the days we used to watch movies in the last week of term or go for class walks or just do fun stuff. Now every lesson is squeezed full of exam prep.

Mr Nolan walks up and down the rows, handing out the papers. He puts mine down on my desk and I pick it up. The exam had been okay I thought. I look but the numbers don't seem right. Sixty per cent. That's … not good.

Perhaps he made a mistake marking it. I tear through the paper, looking for where the marks are, where the mistakes are. Answer: everywhere. Just silly, stupid mistakes. Miscopying numbers, adding up wrongly, equations that don't balance. These aren't mistakes I make…

A fourth A-level was always going to be a stretch – the Head of Sixth Form had warned me about it – but this is basic stuff. I spot where I add seventeen to twenty-four and get thirty-one. My stomach hurts.

Mr Nolan's speaking. 'There was quite a mix of results. Well done to those of you who smashed their targets, and don't give up those who didn't quite reach it this time.'

I feel my face reddening even though no one knows my score. I came nowhere near my predicted grade.

'What did you get?' whispers Rosie.

I can't tell her. 'Not great,' I say. 'You?'

'Sixty-seven per cent! I can't believe it!'

I try and smile but I'm not sure I manage it. Even Rosie's done better than me.

'Let me just say,' Mr Nolan goes on, 'the more work you put in now, the better mark you'll get at the end of next year. I know it feels like a long way off, but it'll be here before you know it.'

I stare at my paper. I did work hard.

Mr Nolan catches my eye, before looking around. 'I know you're all under a lot of pressure, so if any of you need to talk, my door's always open. Right! Let's go through the paper. Question one…'

I zone out. My dad's going to be disappointed. He's always so proud and excited when I get good grades, and he tells all his friends about his clever daughter. It's not that he'll say anything; he'll just *look* disappointed. Like he did when I forgot to make him a Father's Day card. He said it didn't matter, but his eyes. His eyes were sad. And I don't ever want to make him sad.

The lesson ends and everyone crowds towards the door.

'Hetal?' calls Mr Nolan.

'Yes?' I turn back to his desk.

'I know you'll be disappointed with your mark. I'll be honest, it came as a bit of a surprise. Do you know what went wrong? Did something happen on the day of the test?'

I shake my head. There's no excuse.

'Try not to worry too much about it. It's only one exam. I think you understand the topic. It just felt like you weren't quite focussed. Lots of slip-ups.'

'Okay, thanks,' I say. I daren't look at him. I bet he has disappointed eyes too.

I practically run down the corridor and out the door. Good job chemistry is my last lesson. I need to get out of here.

My phone's vibrating somewhere in my bag, so I dig around to find it.

'Hello.' It's Finn. I smile, trying to forget school.

'Hey.'

I can tell by his face something's not right.

'Everything okay?' I ask, putting in my AirPods so no one can hear him but me.

'Yes and no.'

He looks really uncomfortable.

And then I know.

'Look, Hetal, I really like you, but this isn't working. I don't want to hurt you. Knowing you has been the best thing. But I just can't carry on when…' He pauses. 'When you don't seem that interested.'

'What? But I am interested.'

'Really? Okay then. When was the last time you called?'

A long-distance relationship was hard enough without this crap. But then again, I haven't called this week, maybe not last. But I haven't needed to because he's always called first. 'I don't know. I've been busy. And who the hell keeps a record of who calls who and when? Besides, it's on my list to call you.'

He laughs a hollow laugh. 'I'm on the to-do list. Great. That's really great. At least I know this is the right decision. Bye, Hetal.' A beep and he's gone.

I'm left blinking at the blank screen. How dare he? I was going to ring. How can he turn that all on me? I swallow hard. I will not cry here. I *will not*.

This day is all shades of crap. I need to get home. I need to be wrapped in a duvet, with Netflix and snacks. I'm shaking the whole way back.

I walk up the drive, wondering who all the cars belong to. As I go to unlock the front door, Dad opens it.

'Hetal! Brilliant, you're home. Have you got the cake?'

Cake? Oh. The cake.

He can tell by my face that I haven't. They've been planning this get-together for weeks. Nani is seventy and has requested a few friends for a party in the garden. Nothing fancy. Just friends, a cup of tea and ... a piece of cake.

'I'll go and get it now.' I throw my bag into the hall and turn and run back into town. How had I forgotten? Dad reminded me so many times. My eyes are streaming as I run, and I tell myself that everyone will think it's because I'm running so fast. Definitely not because I'm letting everyone down: Finn, Mr Nolan, Dad. I scrub at my eyes.

Nell's not in the deli when I get there. Friday's her college day so thankfully I don't have to explain why I'm late collecting the cake or why my face is blotchy. I peek a look inside the box at the massive cake, covered in a thick creamy icing and an explosion of glittering 70s and happy birthdays. Nani's going to love it. Finally, someone who won't be disappointed in me today.

Why is it all going wrong? I'm trying so hard to please everyone and it's still not working. I grip the box tightly as I start walking back. There's one group of people I don't ever want to let down. I readjust my hold on the box, find my phone and message Sasha, Cam and Nell as I hurry back up the hill.

Can't wait to see you all tomorrow. And can't wait

for the holidays – this trip is going to be The Best! It'll be like old times! X

I can see that Nell's read it – and she's typing a reply.

Can't wait to see everyone tomorrow too – and yay to holidays!

My phone rings. It's Dad.

'Where are you?'

'I'm coming. Only a couple of minutes away.'

Dad sighs. 'Some of Nani's friends have to leave soon and we want to have the cake before they go.'

I hang up and twist to tuck my phone in my pocket, but as I do the cake box slips out of my hand, sails through the air as if in slow motion before landing upside down with a heavy squelch on the pavement.

I groan.

I know without looking it's an ex-cake.

CHAPTER 3
NELL

Saturday

It's Saturday, so the deli is packed with customers. You always get the keen ones, there when the doors open, eager to get the still warm croissants for their weekend brunch. Mid-morning there was nearly a fight over the last custard slice. The customer I was serving and the one Tom was serving both pointed to the last piece at the exact same time. Luckily one of them backed down before it got ugly.

I catch Tom's eye along the counter and smile.

'Have you got one of those poppy seed bloomers?' asks the lady at the front of my queue.

'Yes, of course,' I say, turning to reach one down off the huge display behind me. I'd made them myself this morning and I'm pleased with how they've turned out. Bread making has been my latest rotation at college and we've been studying it for what feels like weeks. My tutor says one of the cornerstones of a good bakery is a decent loaf, so it's worth perfecting, and Wendy has been happy to let me experiment.

I pop the loaf into a paper bag and flick it over to twist the corners. 'Anything else?'

'I'd recommend the sausage rolls,' calls Tom from along the counter. 'The pastry today is especially melt-in-your-mouth.'

The woman smiles and nods to me. 'Can't pass up the opportunity of melt-in-your-mouth pastry. I'll take two.'

I wrap those up for her as well and sort out her change.

I love working here. Wendy, my boss, is amazing. She offered me an apprenticeship so I could carry on working while I go through college. But the thing that really makes the difference (the icing on the cake, lol) is Tom. He's Wendy's nineteen-year-old nephew. Came for a holiday job a couple of years ago and never left.

It's lunchtime and super-busy, with people nearly queueing out of the door. I never take a lunchbreak on a Saturday, there's never time. I catch sight of Cam as she walks past the window. She's hard to miss with her shockingly pink hair. She spots me and squashes her face up against the window and blows out her cheeks. I laugh. I see Cam the most out of our group as she works in town too on the weekends at her foster dad's hardware shop.

Ever since last summer we've been saying we ought to go somewhere, all four of us, and luckily we have Hetal who has actually made sure it's going to happen. And I literally cannot wait. Even though we've not seen too much of each other this year, they're still my best friends. They're the ones who get me, who understand how important this holiday is for me – I was never allowed to go on school trips because my mum always worried. She's much better now. But still. I can't wait for that freedom with my friends.

Tom catches my eye and smiles. We've been seeing each other for a few weeks. Okay five weeks, four days and seventeen hours. Ish.

When I started work at the deli last summer, Tom was going out with Ariel (I know, like the Little Mermaid; what were her parents thinking?) and they'd been together the whole time. She'd sometimes come in after college, or pop in on a

Saturday, and I'd smile and be Very Friendly. But a couple of months ago, things changed. I asked Tom what he and Ariel were doing at the weekend, and he just said, 'Oh, me and Ariel aren't a thing anymore.' Obviously, I had Questions. Which I kept to myself. But this meant Tom was available. And meant the daydreams I'd tried to squash about him came back in technicolour.

Since then, there were Things. Like once, we both reached for the same iced doughnut and brushed fingers. I swear there was an actual spark. I used to look across at him and catch him watching me. The first time he'd looked away quickly, as if he hoped I hadn't seen. The time after that, though, he just smiled and held my gaze. How can a look make you *feel* like that? Like you've run a marathon and your heart's going to jump out of your chest.

It's nearly 4 p.m. We serve until the customers and the fresh produce have gone. Wendy flips the sign on the shop door to *Closed*.

'Great job today. Let's get cleaned up.' She turns on the stereo and music blasts out. It's part of her end-of-day ritual. Today it's *Queen's Greatest Hits* and I love it. We sing and clean until the place is sparkling. I take out the rubbish and give the kitchen one last look round.

Wendy tweaks the display in the window, double-checks she's locked the front door and switches off the lights. Tom and I walk out of the back door, as Wendy locks up behind us.

'Thanks, team,' she says. 'See you tomorrow.'

'Yeah, see you,' I call as she walks away down the back alley to the car park at the bottom of the hill.

Tom's still next to me. 'You got plans this evening?'

'Yeah,' I say. He knows I have.

'Just checking,' he says. 'No way I can persuade you to cancel?'

'And bail on my mates? Not a chance.' I pause. 'But I'm not meeting them until seven.'

He whoops and grabs my hand, pulling me towards the quay.

The sun's still warm as I walk across the little market square, past the bustling pub and along the quayside to the bench. Our bench. Second from the end. Hetal and Cam are already there.

'Hey, Nell,' yells Cam, making an elderly couple frown at her.

I wave back. It always makes me smile that we're so different.

'How's things?' I say as I throw myself down next to them. It's shaded, which is good.

'Everything's fine,' says Hetal. 'At least it's the holidays now. I'm not sure I'd have managed another week.'

'No, me neither,' says Cam. 'And I'm not even doing as much as you are. But time to forget all about it; it's time to chiiiiiillllllll!'

Hetal nods, though she doesn't seem so sure. Wonder what's going on with her?

'Oh, there's Sasha! SASHA!' shouts Cam.

I wave to Sasha as she walks down the quay towards us. She always looks impossibly cool. Most of the time we forget that despite being in our year, she's actually a year older than us; is that why we all look up to her? But thinking back, she's always been this confident.

'Hey, guys,' she says as she gets closer. 'It's so good to see you!'

Cool or not, Cam bear hugs her anyway. She laughs and hugs her back. I wish I could hug people like that. I've worked loads on my confidence this last year, and I am getting better. But still. I feel all clunky and awkward sometimes.

'I really needed that,' she says.

'Bad week?' Hetal asks.

'Just Clarisse and the on-going saga of my dad being totally unreasonable.'

'What's happened now?' We'd heard all about the disastrous dress-fitting and her dad's reaction.

'Clarisse rang. Said Dad wants me at the wedding. Though, thing is, Dad didn't even know Clarisse was ringing. How messed up is that?'

'So, she rang, what, to persuade you to go?' says Hetal.

'I guess.'

'And are you?'

'No.'

'Oh,' says Hetal.

She doesn't say anything else, though it's clear to me and apparently Sasha too, that she has something to say. And I know what.

'Out with it, Hetal,' says Sasha. 'What should I have done?' Her eyebrows are arched, daring Hetal to say.

Hetal shifts uncomfortably on the bench. 'You might not like this.'

Sasha folds her arms. 'Go on.'

Hetal looks around, as if searching for a way to get out of this conversation.

'It's okay, Hetal. I'll say it,' says Cam.

'You know what she's thinking?' Sasha sounds a bit mad now. 'Have you all been talking about me behind my back?'

We totally have.

Cam looks Sasha square in the eyes. 'Don't be daft – of course we have. You're like the only source of drama in our mundane, sad little lives.'

That makes Sasha laugh.

'Thing is, Sash, what happens if you regret it? Not going to the wedding, I mean. What if, in a few months' time, you make things up with your dad? You'll have missed his wedding. You can't get that back. Or what if you never make it up with your dad? What then? Are you really going to throw away your whole relationship with your dad over this? There's like no good outcome here.'

Sasha stares at Cam, the laughter gone. I can't read what she's thinking. Has Cam hurt her? Or has she told Sasha what she already, deep down, knows?

The silence is awkward.

Hetal cracks first.

'So we've got some plans to finalise,' Hetal gabbles, 'before our trip to the Lake District.'

Sasha breaks the eye contact and looks down at her hands, picking at a nail.

We go through Hetal's list confirming we've got everything we need for our Lake District Extravaganza. We've all been saving for months to make it happen, and I can't believe it's nearly here.

Sasha's not saying much – she looks like she's miles away.

'Good,' says Hetal, closing the list on her phone. 'I can go away with my family knowing everything's sorted for when I get back.'

We picked the Tuesday because it would have given Sasha just enough time to get to her dad's wedding and fly back before our trip. I only kind of get why she's not going. Sasha's not really listening to Hetal, like she's still tangled up in her thoughts.

'You're not the only one going on a family trip,' Cam says. 'Sue came into the shop with Maisie and Erin this afternoon. She was talking about how they were going to visit Phil's parents for a few days. And anyway, they've asked me to go with them! Can you believe that? This time last year I didn't even know who my dad was, and now he's taking me to meet my grandparents! It doesn't get any better!'

'What?! That's amazing,' I say. 'They are going to absolutely love you.' And they will – Cam is awesome.

Hetal's hugging Cam hard and I'm grinning. Cam's flushed red and looks like she's about to pop with happiness. It's only Sasha who hasn't reacted.

'Guys. You're right,' Sasha says suddenly. Everyone looks at her. 'I've got to be at that wedding. Thanks for the reminder about how important it is. It doesn't matter who he's marrying, he's still my dad.'

And now it's Sasha's turn to be hugged.

'Sasha, I'm so pleased for you,' says Hetal once the hugging is done. 'When's your flight?'

'Flight? Oh, crap. I cancelled it.'

Hetal starts tapping away on her phone. 'When's the wedding again?'

'A week tomorrow. Sunday,' she says. 'I should have just kept the tickets.'

'Are you going to ring your dad and tell him?' I ask, thinking he might help with tickets.

Sasha thinks for moment. 'No, I don't think so. I don't want him to say anything that might make me change my mind. Best to surprise him on the day and try and patch things up while he's floating on the wave of wedding vibes.'

'Erm, Sasha,' says Hetal, looking up from her phone. 'Hate to say it, but there aren't many seats available going to Marseille in the next few days and the ones left are *really* expensive. Like four figures expensive.'

'Okay, okay. That's no problem. I'll just have to find another way. What about the train? That could work?'

We're all on our phones now, desperately searching.

'Trains are super-expensive. It's last minute and a really long way. It would be okay if it was Northern France, but it's way down on the south coast,' says Cam, scrolling. 'Have you a bike perhaps? If you set off now, you should make it in five days' time.'

We all laugh.

'What about driving?' I ask. 'If your mum would let you borrow her car.'

It's a big if.

Hetal's searching. 'Hmmm. Okay. That might be doable. The ferry isn't too much and then it would just be fuel and accommodation on the way.'

Cam claps her hands. 'You could camp! We've already got the kit.'

That might actually work. If anyone has the confidence to drive through France, it's Sasha.

'Ring your mum. See what she says,' Cam urges.

Her mum answers after four rings. 'Hey, honey. Everything okay?'

'Yeah, everything's fine. I've changed my mind about Dad's wedding. I want to go.'

'I think that's a very mature decision.' We can hear her smiling.

'Only thing is the flights are crazy expensive. Trains, too. So, I was wondering…' Sasha pauses. We all lean in, trying to hear what she's going to say.

'Are you wanting to borrow my car and drive?'

There's a touch less smile in her voice now.

'It won't be for long, and I promise I'll drive carefully.'

She's silent and we all wait. It doesn't help to rush Sasha's mum.

'Okay then. But on one condition. You can't go on your own. It's a long way and it would be safer with someone else.'

'You're not suggesting … you, are you?'

'Goodness me, no. Last person your father wants at his wedding.' She chuckles. 'What are your friends doing this week?'

Sasha looks round at us. Hetal is away with her family and Cam is meeting her grandparents. Everyone looks at me.

'I'll have to check with Mum and Dad, and Wendy,' I say, quickly running scenarios in my head. Then I grin. 'But I can't see how they're going to stop me!'

Sasha gives me a massive hug. 'Thanks, Nell. Mum, Nell has volunteered.'

'Okay then love. We'll talk about the details later.'

'Thanks, Mum! You're the best,' says Sasha before finishing the call. She's grinning at me and I'm grinning back! A road trip through France with Sasha! Oh. My. Goodness. This is taking freedom to the next level. Hope Mum doesn't freak out.

Hetal is quiet. Staring at her phone.

'Hetal?' says Cam. 'Everything okay?'

Hetal looks up. 'I've been doing some quick calculations. Distance to travel, how much you could safely drive in a day, that sort of thing.'

'And?' I say. 'We should have loads of time to get there. The wedding's not until Sunday.'

'That's not the problem.'

'What is then?' asks Cam.

'You won't be back in time for our Lake District trip.'

CHAPTER 4
CAM

Monday

I'm gutted the Lake District trip is off. I can't believe we're not going to get our holiday all together. Hetal looked devastated the other night but she didn't say anything. Just that she'd make sure everything she'd booked was cancelled so we could get our money back.

I had thought about not going to meet my grandparents and going with Sasha and Nell instead. But I couldn't do that to Hetal, leave her out like that – she's got a family holiday she says she can't get out of. And besides, grandparents don't come along every day and I've got to be realistic.

I'm seventeen. I'm in foster care, and that

finishes when I'm eighteen. At eighteen everything gets very real, very fast, so I'd be lying if I said I wasn't thinking about my support network. My foster parents, Papa John and Jackie are awesome and have said that they'll help for as long as I need it. But I'm not an idiot. Foster caring is their job, and they'll have to take in another young person. This is where having a proper family is going to really help. Not that I want to live with them or anything. I know I'm going to have to be independent. It just feels a bit lonely. A bit scary too, if I'm honest.

I muss up my pink hair in the hallway mirror, jam my sunglasses on top of my head and pace. I'm waiting for Phil, Sue and the girls to pick me up. I didn't sleep last night. My mind wouldn't stop. But I don't care. Today's the day I get to see my real-life completely-mine grandparents for the first time.

'Have you got everything you need?' asks Jackie. 'Sun cream, some cool clothes as it looks like the weather's due to be warm?'

'Yep and yep. I am totally set.'

'And you've got the box of chocolates? Remember they're a gift, not for you to eat in the car!' Anyone would think Jackie is as excited as I am about seeing them.

'Yes!'

'It'll take them a bit of time to get used to the idea of having a very nearly grown-up granddaughter. Don't rush them.'

'Yes, I know. Take it steady, don't assume. I've done this before, remember? And besides. They're Phil's mum and dad – they're bound to be lovely.'

Jackie nods and smiles. 'I'm sure they will be.'

Papa John comes into the hallway. 'You still here?'

He's joking.

'I hope you have a smashing few days.' He gives me one of his speciality bear hugs.

'I will do.'

I check the time on the hall clock. They're late. We should have left fifteen minutes ago. Then a car pulls up outside and toots its horn.

'That's them!' I yank open the front door and run out but have to come back for my stuff. Even with the doors closed I can hear Maisie and Erin shouting my name. Phil takes my bags off me and squeezes them into an already stuffed boot.

Jackie gives me a hug and Papa John shakes Phil's hand and I wriggle into the back seat between Maisie and Erin.

'We've got snacks and games and oh my

goodness this is going to be so amazing,' gabbles Maisie.

Erin is grinning hard as she grips my hand with her little one.

'Let's go, Dad,' calls Maisie. 'Gran and Gramps will be waiting for us.'

Phil finishes off chatting to Papa John and Jackie and jumps into the driver's seat. 'Everyone ready?'

'RREEEEAAAADDDYYYY,' yell Maisie and Erin.

Sue turns in her seat. 'I'm afraid they're a little over-excited.'

'That's fine,' I say. 'So am I!'

As we travel along miles and miles of motorway, I watch *Mulan* over Maisie's shoulder. Erin's been asleep for a while now. I'm so close to meeting my grandparents. I've already missed years and years of knowing them. And, not being funny, I don't know what their health is like. There might not be a lot of years left.

The girls have been brilliant. Sasha gave me the biggest hug. Hetal sent me an article she'd found on tips for meeting family for the first time, highlighting various sections. She said it was because she knows I wouldn't be bothered to read the whole thing, so she'd picked out the key points. Nell simply texted this morning: *Be yourself. If that doesn't work, they don't deserve you.* Which was sweet.

I fidget in my seat, trying not to wake Erin. We can't be far away. Phil said they live somewhere near London, and we're off the motorway and driving through a really built-up area. There seems to be no break between towns.

'You okay back there?' says Sue.

'Yeah,' I say.

'We're not far away now, about another five minutes.'

Excitement tingles through me like a current. I'm finally getting to meet them. I've seen photos of them – there's one of them sitting on a garden bench together hung on the wall at Phil and Sue's house. Neither of them are very smiley, but photos don't always capture your best.

Phil swings the car into a small drive and parks in front of a house with roses around the front door. It. Is. Perfect.

Erin stirs and Maisie starts stuffing her things frantically back into her bag. 'We're here, we're here, we're here,' she sings.

I'm suddenly nervous. I smooth out my top and flatten my hair. Perhaps I should have chosen a more natural shade for this visit. Toxic Pink perhaps isn't quite the right vibe.

Phil and Sue swap a look, then get out of the car. Phil opens the back door. Maisie jumps out and Erin scrambles across me in her desperation. I follow.

The front door is flung open and two people come out. It's them. Exactly like the photo, only they both look a bit older. And they're smiling.

I smile too. This is going to be okay.

Phil's mum is hugging Maisie, and Phil's dad is swinging Erin up in the air and both girls are giddy with giggles.

'Hi, Mum,' says Phil, kissing his mother on the cheek.

Phil's dad sideways hugs Sue. 'Lovely to see you all again. Wonderful to have you.'

I wait. No one can ignore Maisie and Erin when they're like this. And Phil and Sue haven't seen Phil's parents in ages. And it's lovely to watch all the hugging. It won't be long until I'm included in the welcome.

'Well, then. Come along in,' says Phil's mum. 'We've got cakes in the kitchen.'

Maisie and Erin squeal in excitement and disappear inside.

'How was the journey?' Phil's dad asks him, and they walk in together. Sue follows.

I hesitate, still standing by the car.

Phil's mum turns to me.

I wait, holding my breath, waiting to meet my grandmother.

'Perhaps you could bring in the bags?'

And she turns on her heel and walks into the house.

Had I heard wrong? I shake my head a little. Should I bring in the bags? It would give everyone time to catch up. I don't want to intrude on that, I guess.

I open the boot and lift out bag after bag, carrying them and stacking them in the hallway. I'm nearly finished when Phil comes out.

'Oh, there you are. I wondered where you'd got to.' He looks at the nearly empty boot. 'You didn't have to do that. But thank you.'

'No worries,' I say.

'You're not too nervous, are you? I realised we all ran in and left you. It must feel very weird to be here.'

'Yeah, it does. I'm trying to be cool about it though. It's just a pretty big deal.'

'Of course, it is. Let's lock up the car and I'll

introduce you properly. It'll be fine.' His eyes don't meet mine, and he fiddles around with his car keys. Is he nervous too?

I follow Phil into the house, through the hall and into a large, sunny kitchen. Maisie and Erin are both sat up to the table, a big slice of cake in front of each of them.

'Cam!' Maisie calls. 'You've got to try Gran's cake. It's amazing. The bestest cake in the whole entire world.'

'It does look amazing,' I say.

I notice Phil's mum putting the lid back on a big cake tin. She's not offering me a piece?

Phil clears his throat. 'Mum, Dad, I'd like to introduce you to Cam, Camille. Cam, these are your grandparents.'

Maisie and Erin grin. Sue is smiling at Phil's parents encouragingly.

'Not the proper way to introduce a granddaughter,' sniffs his mother. 'Usually, you get to meet them *much* sooner. But I understand that someone didn't see fit to share the news that my son had become a father.'

I'm hearing the words but struggling to understand. Is she having a go at my mum? A wave of pain and anger rises from inside. How dare she!

'I thought we'd take the children to the park,' she goes on. 'Give you two a break. You've been working so hard.'

Maisie and Erin are cheering and scrambling out of their chairs.

'We'll be back in a bit.' And Phil's parents sweep Maisie and Erin out of the kitchen and out of the house.

I look at Phil, then Sue, searching for confirmation that this was a bit messed up, but they're busy with sorting out bags and making another cup of tea.

I've got this horrible feeling that coming here wasn't such a good idea.

CHAPTER 5
SASHA

Monday

Snacks, tent, sleeping bag, pillow, clothes, make-up, phone, charger, map book (Mum's idea not mine; that's what Google Maps is for).

I look around my room. What have I forgotten?

'Sasha,' Mum calls from downstairs. 'Hetal's here.'

I pick up my bags in one hand, tuck my sleeping bag under an arm and grab my phone. Why's Hetal here?

'Hey,' says Hetal when I get downstairs. She looks downbeat. 'Thought I'd come and see you off. And give you this.' She hands over a folder.

It's packed with print-offs and timetables.

'It's colour coded,' she says. 'Blue for campsites, green for daytrips, yellow for grocery shops, red for nearest hospitals. I think I've got everything.'

I flick through the folder and whistle. 'This is awesome! And it must have taken you ages. Wow. Thank you.' I hug her.

'I wish I was coming.'

She looks totally gutted. I get it. We're missing out on our holiday all together because of this. 'I wish you were coming, too. But you'll have a brilliant holiday with your family. Promise to send photos. I want to see you doing karaoke with your Nani!'

Hetal manages a smile. 'And I want to see photos too. Of everything.'

The doorbell rings.

'That'll be Nell,' I say and go to let her in. She's on the doorstep with a pile of bags roughly the same size as mine.

Hetal walks up behind me. 'How big is your mum's car again?'

Nell laughs. 'I don't think there exists a car big enough!'

Hetal claps her hands. 'Okay. You've got to start with the essentials and see how far you get. What's the most essential thing?'

'Phone,' we both say, and laugh.

Hetal rolls her eyes. 'Let's assume we'll be able to find room for your phones. What else?'

'Tent,' I say. 'Definitely fairly essential for a camping holiday.'

Hetal goes out to the car and lifts the tent into the boot. The boot suddenly looks full. This could be trickier than I thought.

'Remember it's just the two of us,' says Nell. 'We can fill up the back seat.'

'I think you're being over-optimistic about the size of the back seat,' says Hetal, eyeing our piles of luggage. 'You need to face the reality of leaving some of this stuff behind.'

I start going through my bags. It all feels so essential. 'How many pairs of shoes would you say?'

Hetal and Nell think for a moment.

'Something comfy to walk in, something fancy if you go out, maybe something if it's wet?' says Hetal counting off on her fingers. 'So, three.'

I open my bag wide, and they peer in. 'So not seven then?'

Nell giggles and opens her bag up and takes out pair after pair. 'Twelve,' she says. 'If you include flip flops.'

'I think you may need a car just for footwear,' says Hetal.

'How about the back seat is for shoes,' I suggest, thinking that twelve pairs is perhaps *a little* excessive.

Hetal's shaking her head. 'No. Back seat must be clear. If you leave your car anywhere, you want any would-be thieves to think the car is empty. Everything has to fit in the boot.'

We agree on leaving some stuff behind and manage to get the car packed to Hetal's standard. I wish she was coming with us. She knows so much life stuff. I flick through the folder she's given me again.

'There's a list of postcodes to put into Google Maps to get the right directions,' says Hetal.

'I won't need to navigate then?' says Nell.

'Technically, no,' says Hetal, 'but it's always good having a second set of eyes.'

I start to feel nervous. I'm fine at driving, passed first time and not had an accident, but this will be driving in France. On the right-hand side of the road. Are the road signs different? 'Yeah, definitely helpful to have someone else checking I'm going the right way.'

'No problem,' says Nell, grinning. 'Though is it really a road trip if we don't get lost?'

Hetal faux gasps. 'I haven't mapped out every

journey including picnic spots, toilets and things to look out for along the route just for you to get lost!'

We all laugh.

'Seriously. I wish I was coming.'

She looks so sad, that I hug her tight. Nell's half-hugging her too. It's all because of me that we're not getting our summer together. Hetal's not saying out loud that she blames me, but it's there, for everyone to see.

'Right.' Hetal pulls out of the hug and checks her phone. 'As much as I don't want you to go, I think it's time you did. Don't want to miss the ferry check-in.'

Got to love her, always so practical.

Mum goes on about sticking to the speed limits and remembering to put my lights on when I'm driving at night and not letting what's happening in the car distract me from driving.

'I'll be careful,' I say.

'And have a lovely time at the wedding.'

I hug her. I can't tell her now that I'm worried about going. What if Dad doesn't want me there? Or I completely mess up the whole thing and ruin it for him? Everyone's changed their plans for me. I can't now say I'm having second thoughts.

Hetal's helping Nell adjust the passenger seat.

'Oh good, I haven't missed you!' Tom arrives, out-of-breath. He must have run all the way from the deli. 'Wendy said I could pop out to see you off.'

Hetal catches my eye and we both pretend we're very interested in something inside, so Nell and Tom can have a moment. But after a few minutes, and there's still no sign of Nell being ready to leave, I cough loudly and step outside.

'Okay, then,' I say loudly, getting into the driver's seat. 'Time to go.'

Nell hugs Tom tightly.

'Hope you have a wonderful time,' Mum calls.

'Remember to send photos,' calls Hetal. 'I want it to feel like I'm actually there.'

Nell gets into the car beside me.

'All set?' I ask.

We drive away down the road. I can see Mum, Hetal and Tom all madly waving in the rear-view mirror. Nell is waving back out of her window. It's hard leaving Hetal behind.

We turn the corner, and they disappear out of sight.

'Road trip of a lifetime, here we come!' I whoop.

'I'll sort some music,' Nell says. 'Hetal's sent a link to a playlist.'

Within seconds we've got loud music, windows

down and the road stretching out in front of us. I'm glad Nell's with me but I'm sad it's not all four of us.

There's a loud metal clanging as I drive across the gangplank and onto the ferry. The air's thick with diesel fumes and the floor's thrumming making the whole car, and us in it, shake.

We're really doing this.

Nell turns the music down so I can concentrate. There's a man in hi-vis waving us forward, forward, forward, stop! I turn off the engine and exhale.

'Phew. That was tight.'

'You did brilliantly, though.'

I grin at her. 'Thanks. Right. Let's go and explore. I hear there's even a cinema on board.'

'Really?'

'According to Hetal's notes!'

We go up floor after floor of noisy metal steps until we get to the deck which has shops on it. We check the deck plan. It feels kind of weird that there are almost as many things to do on this ship as there are in our town: dozens of little shops, a cinema and even a gym!

'What do you want to do first?'

'You choose,' says Nell.

I scan through the options. 'Okay. Food, then

cinema, but first, let's go out on deck and watch as we set off. I've never seen a ship this large leave a dock before.'

We push hard on a heavy door and the wind whips our breath away. It's brilliant sunshine and we go and stand at the barriers, watching as huge iron chains are wound in and the engines roar into life. A blast from the ship's horn and we gradually edge away from the dock.

'Wooooohoooooo!' I shout into the air. The thrill of having a few days of freedom is buzzing through me. Wedding or no wedding, this is going to be a trip to remember.

CHAPTER 6
HETAL

Middle of Monday night

We had all agreed. It was more important for Sasha to go to her father's wedding. She'd cried on Saturday when it was decided, and said she loved us all. I hadn't cried until I got home. We're missing our trip and, while I'm so happy for Sasha, my heart is breaking for all the plans we've made that we're not getting to do.

I'd told Sasha and Nell I'd make all the plans for their trip. Sasha seemed to be so distracted by everything and Nell didn't say much, so it felt like the obvious thing to do. I am the 'organiser' of the group after all. I'd booked their ferry and felt pretty chuffed at the deal I found, though it was a bit weird, organising a trip I'm not going on. I've done nothing since Saturday night except research campsites, tourist attractions and routes through France. A careful balance of nice places to stay, interesting places to see and it not costing the earth. And of course, making sure they get to the wedding in time. I've made sure this trip is perfect.

Perhaps the upside is now I have an unexpected free week to catch up on study after our family holiday. The work this last year at school has been insane: hours every night, every weekend. And I do need to do some work over the holidays.

It doesn't feel much like an upside.

I was so looking forward to being with everyone. I feel out of touch. Not big-time. We haven't argued or anything. It's like we've fallen out of step with each other, and it would have been so good to talk and hang out and be together for more than just an evening.

I check my phone instinctively. I know there won't be any messages now, but I can't stop checking. I've not heard from Finn since Friday, and it feels weird. He used to send me funny clips of animals, and little messages in the evenings, and I hadn't realised how much that had become part of my day. And I miss it. I miss him. Another good reason why I needed that holiday. I seriously have to get my head out of this funk. I need to get up, dust off and move on. I look over at my neat folder of Lake District plans lying on my desk.

I check my phone again without thinking. Crap. How desperate am I? Throwing my phone to the other end of my bed, I vow not to look at it for the next ten minutes.

I can't sleep. I've tried lying still with my eyes shut. I've tried sleep sounds. I've tried counting backwards from one hundred. I've even tried thinking of an animal for every letter of the alphabet.

And I didn't even manage that. I had to Google if a Xolo counts (it does).

It's 2.30 a.m. I'm wide awake. And all I can think about is Sasha and Nell. I click open my phone and look at the selfie they sent. Both grinning. Sun shining. Zero worries.

I wish I was with them. I wish we were going on holiday all together. Lake District. France. It doesn't matter.

I allow myself to sit with the ache of sadness.

So why aren't I with them?

I turn over and adjust my pillow.

My family. I've disappointed them enough. I'm not about to let them down again.

My tummy rumbles. Perhaps if I go downstairs and have a snack, I'll be able to sleep.

I slip out of bed, creep out of my room and go downstairs. I can hear my dad snoring, even though their door is closed. Once downstairs I fridge-gaze, wondering what to have.

'I thought I heard someone down here.'

I jump. 'Nani! You scared the life out of me,' I whisper.

'Sorry.'

I can hear her smiling in the gloom of the kitchen.

'Can't sleep?'

'No. And then I got the munchies. So here I am. How about you?'

'Fancied a cuppa. Want one?'

Tea? In the middle of the night? How often does she do this?

'Yeah, why not. Thanks, Nani.'

I find some cheese and some fancy chutney, make myself a sandwich and sit at the table. Nani puts down two mugs of tea and sits opposite me.

I spent a whole day looking at pictures of France, studying routes, researching the best places to see, the best deals for campsites and the ones with the best views. And I won't get to see any of it. I put all our favourite tunes into a playlist called

Musique de road trip en France, but I'll never listen to it there. Sasha and Nell are in France: they put up their tent, ate overlooking the sea and said it was so warm they could leave the flaps open on the tent so they could see the stars as they went to sleep. I know this because they've sent a bazillion photos and told me every detail. I'm so desperate to be there it's making my body hurt. Like all my limbs are stone-heavy and my stomach is full of concrete.

'You okay?' asks Nani.

'Yes. Fine.'

'All packed for the morning?'

'Nearly.'

'Any plans for the week?'

'No.'

'You usually have a whole itinerary.'

I shrug. 'Not this time.'

'You know, when I can't sleep, I watch my quiz show.' Nani sets up her iPad between us and presses play. 'So far, I'm outperforming these contestants by double. They didn't even know the capital of the US. I mean, where do they find these people?'

I watch with her. She's calling out all the answers way before anyone else does.

I've got to stop thinking about France and the road trip. I remind myself I'm lucky to be going on holiday with my family. Loads of people don't get holidays or don't have families that love them. I wonder how Cam is getting on. It's her first night with her grandparents. It's weird I've not heard from her. Does that mean it's going well? I hope so. I can't even begin to imagine not having met your own grandparents before. I look across at Nani and think how lucky I am.

Nani turns off the tablet.

Has the quiz show finished?

'You must think I'm daft.'

What? 'Of course I don't. You're getting way more answers than I am.'

'Forget the quiz. I mean you. You say you're fine. But it's obvious something's bothering you. So come on. Out with it.'

You really can't fool Nani.

'It's nothing really.'

'But there is a thing?'

'No. Yes. Sort of. Sasha and Nell left to go on their road trip.'

'And…?'

I swallow. 'And I wish I was with them.' Then I gabble, 'But it's not that I don't want to come on holiday with you – it's going to be great. It's just…' I trail off.

Nani narrows her eyes at me, like she's trying to read my mind. 'And what about Cam? What's she up to?'

'She's meeting her grandparents for the first time. But that was all a bit last minute too.'

'And your Lake District holiday is definitely off?'

I nod. 'I cancelled all our bookings today.'

Nani doesn't say anything else, just flicks her tablet back on, though I notice she's no longer shouting out the answers. I quietly finish eating my sandwich. When the show's over, she turns it off.

'Obviously I want you to come away with us.'

'I know, Nani. That's why I'm here.'

'Ah my sweet, lovely girl.' She pats my arm. 'But there is one thing I want more.'

I frown. What can that be?

'I want you to be happy. *You.*'

'I am! I'm happy when you are.'

Nani laughs. 'You're always so thoughtful. Do you know what would make me the happiest? Seeing you do the things you love, being with those you love. Living your life. A life with no regrets. And while I would treasure you coming with us on holiday, I could never forgive myself if you had to miss a road trip with your friends. I mean. That's serious … what do you young people call it … life goals?'

I smile. 'Yeah. Road tripping with friends is serious life goals.'

'What I'm saying is, if you want to be with your friends, then that's what I want too.'

'But what about this holiday? Besides, Sasha and Nell have already left.'

'Forget the family holiday. And as for them having already set off, I've seen you with a timetable. Don't tell me you can't find a way to catch them up!'

I shake my head. 'Nani, I can't disappoint you. Or Dad, or Mum. I just couldn't bear it.'

She leans across the table and cups my chin in her hands. 'My Hetal. Life is full of disappointments. If you never disappoint others, you'll only end up disappointing yourself. Besides, the only way you're going to disappoint me is if you hold any part of yourself back. I want you to be happy and free and following your heart. No regrets.'

My brain is on fire. Maybe I could go. But they're already in France. How do I get to them?

I lean over and hug Nani tight.

Then I remember the holiday had been chosen with me in mind. 'Oh no! Dad said the resort you're staying at has a young vibe.'

Nani chuckles. 'Good job I'm young at heart then. It's been years since I've danced till midnight!'

I laugh. Nani is going to be more than fine! She'll show everyone how to party. My head's swirling. I'm going on the road trip! I get to see Sasha and Nell. I get to visit all the places I've been planning. I get to go on the road trip of a lifetime! Now all I have to do is work out how to get there.

CHAPTER 7
NELL

Tuesday

I'm woken by the sound of children playing. The sun's shining through the tent fabric and it's deliciously warm; it feels like I'm snuggled into a cloud. Sasha's snoring in the pod next to mine. I can't believe I'm here, away from home. It's not exactly how our trip was supposed to go; obviously it would be loads better with Hetal and Cam here. But the freedom. Not having someone telling you what you should be doing and when. Us deciding where we go, what we eat, when we sleep. It feels amazing.

I reach for my phone and check for messages. There are loads. Three are from Tom which I read quickly, the casual 'x' at the end of every text making me smile. I reply, knowing he's probably already at the deli by now. Feels odd not being there with him. I move onto the others which are *all* from Hetal. And she's not making a lot of sense.

I have some AMAZING news!

Call me the minute you wake up.

Are you awake yet?

I can't wait. The news is I CAN COME ON THE ROAD TRIP WITH YOU!

AAAGGGGHHHHHH!

Why aren't you awake yet? Oh. Yeah. It's half-six with you. Could be the reason. Lol!

But seriously. Call me.

CCAAAAALLLLLL MMMMMEEEEEE!

I do as I'm instructed and call. She picks up after one ring.

'Nell! Hi! Can you believe it? I can come with you! I'm so excited. This is going to be the most awesome thing EVER.'

'Hetal! Slow down. You're not making any sense. What happened to your family holiday?'

'Nani sorted it. Said she would prefer me to be happy and on the road trip than coming along to keep her happy. Can you believe her? She's the absolute best.'

Hetal's Nani is awesome. When we all went to Paris last year, she treated us all like her grandkids.

'Oh my GOODNESS! That's so brilliant! Okay, what's the plan?'

Sasha unzips her pod. 'Why can I hear Hetal? Hetal? Is that you?'

We both laugh. 'I'm chatting with her now – and she's got some awesome news. You tell her, Hetal.'

Sasha crawls into my pod and flops onto the lilo next to me. 'What news, Hetal?'

'I can come on the road trip!'

Sasha screams. 'Yessss! That's brilliant. How's that going to work?'

'I'm still figuring out the details, but I'm hoping to catch the train and get there later today. Think I've found a deal that makes it cheaper.'

Both me and Sasha scream this time.

'Today? That's insane! Let us know when and where and we can meet you. This is going to be brilliant!'

Hetal's beaming. 'I'd better go. Lots to organise. I'll let you know all the details as soon as they're sorted. See you soon!'

'Bye!' we both shout as Hetal hangs up.

'I can't believe it, Hetal's road-tripping with us

after all – this is amazing,' says Sasha. 'So, if she's coming later, what shall we do with our day?'

'Let's see what Hetal recommends,' I say, leaning into the shared living space and grabbing the itinerary. 'Hmmmm. There are quite a few options for Saint Malo – seafront, marketplace, walk round the town walls, explore the old town. Hold on. There's a creperie with outstanding reviews. Fancy that?'

'Sounds perfect.'

Half an hour later we zip up our tent and walk towards the town centre. It's not too warm yet, but the air feels like it's brewing a scorcher. Yesterday didn't really count as the first day – I always feel kind of shell-shocked at the start of a holiday, but today my brain's clearer and I can take it all in: the busy streets, the snippets of conversations in French, the signs I only half understand.

'I can't believe Hetal's coming,' says Sasha. We're walking along the seafront. It's so still today, barely a wave, hardly a puff of breeze.

'I know! It's amazing. Kind of feel bad that Cam can't come though. Hope she doesn't feel too left out.'

'Yeah. But she's meeting her grandparents for the first time. That's pretty awesome.'

We turn away from the sea and along one of the cobbled streets, through an archway in the thick stone wall casting cool dark shadows, before walking into the old town. It's bustling with people. You can spot the tourists a mile off, just like at home. Though I guess we're like them now. I wish I was with Tom. We'd play our game of guessing where they're from. It's not homesickness I'm feeling; I'm missing a person, not a place. Is people-sickness a thing?

I check my phone. No messages. He's read the last one I sent but hasn't replied. I know he's at work, so probably read it quickly and didn't have time to reply, but still. There's a bit of me that's disappointed.

'Take a photo,' calls Sasha. She's perched on the edge of a fountain, classic model pose, turned sideways and hair thrown back.

I take a few shots, then go over to show her.

'These are brilliant,' she says, swiping through them.

'You're photogenic,' I say but she bats away the compliment.

'No, you've got a real eye for framing.'

I lean in to see what she's saying. As we're both peering at the screen, a message pops up. It's from Tom.

Sorry didn't have time to reply earlier. Crazy busy at the deli. Queue out of the door! Aunt Wendy has asked someone to help out, just while you're away. Missing you.

We both read it.

'That's good. That they've got someone in to help,' says Sasha.

Is it though? I nibble my bottom lip and wonder if the replacement person will be better than me. What if the customers like them more, they're faster at serving, better at baking.

I read the message again and start to reply.

There's a shout and a large ball of floof runs across the square.

'Arreter! Oh toi villain chien!'

The dog leaps towards me, a red tongue hanging out of the side of its mouth like the whole thing is a massive joke. He jumps up at me, licking my face and making me stumble. I lose my balance; the low wall bangs into the back of my knees. I tip, then plunge backwards into the fountain.

The water's freezing but luckily not very deep. I scramble to my feet, gasping at the sudden coldness.

'Pardon! Est-ce que ca va?'

My French isn't too bad. I got a 6 at GCSE. But

it turns out if I'm soaked in fountain water, all my French skills dissolve. Sasha's not much use. She's bent over laughing, though has held it together long enough to be filming me. Classic friend.

Then I realise. My phone.

It was in my hand. I look around me and spot it, resting on a layer of coins at the bottom of the pool.

I fish it out and look at it, pressing the screen, desperately hoping it works.

It doesn't. It's totally dead.

CHAPTER 8
CAM

Tuesday

I check my clothes and hair in the mirror, mussing up my hair and shaking back my shoulders. I am bigger than this.

Today is going to be better.

It can't be any worse.

My phone's useless. There's no signal here, and my grandfather says they don't give out their wifi password because they like to keep it 'secure'. I'd laughed until I realised he was serious.

Maisie and Erin are already downstairs, laughing and chatting in the kitchen. They must have been up for ages. Phil's parents are so lovely with them. I heard his mum say she'd got their favourite cereal in and got out their favourite toys. And that's wonderful. For Maisie and Erin. Not so much for me. They can be nice, which means they're choosing not to be. Would it be easier if they were horrid to everyone? My heart breaks at the thought of Maisie and Erin losing out on lovely grandparents. No, I don't wish they were nasty to everyone.

I will not let this situation get to me. I won't let it hurt me. I haven't done anything wrong. I try to hang onto Nell's words that they're lucky to know me, but it's hard when they seem to really hate me.

I walk down to the kitchen, a smile forced onto my face. Phil's not here. Nor is Sue.

'Caammmm,' squeals Maisie when she sees me. She runs across the room to hug me around the waist. 'You were asleep for ages! Come and see what we're doing.'

I allow her to lead me across the kitchen to the table where I admire their drawings – they're pretty good actually. Maisie likes portraits and she's labelled everyone, which certainly helps you to know who's who!

'I love these,' I say. 'You've got Erin's eyes spot-on.'

Maisie swells with pride. 'They took me a really

long time.' She looks sad. 'But Gran doesn't have a pink, so I can't do your hair.'

I look up, into my grandmother's eyes. She's got an eyebrow raised. Then I look at the huge colouring pen set. There must be fifty colours. 'No pink, huh? Wow, that's bad luck. You would have thought a fancy colouring set like this would have had at least one pink.'

Maisie frowns. 'Yes, that is odd.'

My grandmother clears her throat. 'Let's not worry too much about that. Let's think about what we've got planned today.'

Maisie and Erin both gaze up at her, eyes wide, full of trust that this woman holds the answers to all their dreams. I remember my gran. Gran who gathered me up after Mum died. Told me I was everything to her. Made me believe I was someone worth loving. I remember loving her like this. It pinches at my heart.

'First, we're going to put away the breakfast things because it's way past breakfast time. And then we're going to go down to the boating lake. Gramps has booked a boat for the six of us and we'll pack up a picnic and go sailing for the day.'

Maisie's looking puzzled. 'Why does the boat only have room for six people? There is me and

Erin and you and Gramps and Mummy and Daddy and Cam. That's seven.'

'Ah, well we'd booked it before we knew she was coming. And we knew you'd still want to go on the boat. It's only for the day. I'm sure she'll find something else to do.'

I know without a shadow of doubt that this woman hates me. Hates what I've done to her perfect family. Hates that I'm in her family. No, scrub that, she's still in denial that I'm even in it. She can't even bring herself to say my name. The feeling's mutual. The word *gran* has been stuck in my throat since I got here. My gran was kind and generous and loved me so fiercely that I can still feel it burning in the universe. Nothing like this woman. To call this woman Gran? I'd rather choke.

I open my mouth to say something, to bite back, but I catch Maisie and Erin looking up at me now, eyes worried. There's another love that's bright and fierce. I can't hurt them. I swallow my words. Bite my tongue.

'That's alright,' I say, crouching down so I'm talking to Maisie and Erin. 'Don't worry. I'll be fine, and when you get back you can tell me all about it. Okay?'

The worry lines smooth on Maisie's face. 'Okay.'

It should be okay. I'll have the day to myself; perhaps I can chill and binge-watch something. It's all got too claustrophobic for me.

'Now, off you run and tell Mummy and Daddy the plan while I sort out the food,' says my grandmonster.

The girls run out of the room, shouting about boats and picnics.

The smile snaps off my grandmonster's face. 'I'd prefer it if you weren't in our house on your own. So, if you could get yourself ready to go out for the day?'

'What? Wow. What exactly do you think I'm going to do?'

She raises her pencilled eyebrows. 'Who knows? Who knows what your sort would do. All I know is I'm not prepared to leave someone I don't know in our home without close supervision.'

'My sort? What sort is that, exactly? You may or may not like the idea, but I am *literally* your sort. I'm your granddaughter and there is nothing you can do about that. Sorry you seem to hate the idea so very much. But sure. No problem. I'll get out of your house.' My blood is raging in my veins.

I storm out of the kitchen and up the stairs. I stuff my clothes back into my bag, yank my charger out of the wall and leave the room, slamming the door behind me.

'What's going on?' says Phil, coming out of the sitting room.

'Ask your mother,' I mutter as I walk past him towards the front door.

His next words get obliterated by the door slamming behind me.

I throw my bag onto my shoulder, walk down the drive and onto the road without a backward glance.

My whole body is ridged with fury, hands balled into fists and shoulders hunched. How dare she? What a poisonous woman. How could she treat her own granddaughter like that? But she doesn't see me as her granddaughter. She just sees a misfit. A sob escapes. I scrub at my eyes. I won't waste my tears on her. She's not worth it.

But the tears keep coming. And I keep walking. I want as much distance as I possibly can get between us.

My phone buzzes in my pocket. I ignore it.

After about twenty minutes I'm out of tears and out of breath. I stop at a junction, trying to figure out where I am. I haven't a clue.

Right. What's the plan, Cam?

I sit on a low garden wall. What are my options? I could go back, say I'm sorry and get walked all over.

Not going to happen.

The alternative? Go home. Tell Jackie that it didn't work out. She'd know what to do.

What I wouldn't give for one of Papa John's bear hugs right now.

I pull out my phone. There's an insane number of messages on the group chat. I'm itching to read them but I should probably check my other messages first. I'll catch up on the road trip and Hetal's holiday later.

There are four missed calls from Phil, one from Jackie and a voicemail.

I click play.

'Cam. It's Phil. I don't know what's happened, but please come back. We can sort it out. We can sort anything out. Just please. Come back. Or at least call me. Please.'

I press delete. We can't sort this out.

I call Jackie instead.

'Cam? Everything okay?'

I can tell from her voice that she's worried. Phil must have called her already.

'Yeah. Well, no, actually. I'm coming home.'

'Ah, love. Of course, that's fine. Want to tell me what's happened?'

I swallow hard. I need to say my grandmother

hates me but the words are stuck in my throat. 'I'll tell you when I get home. I just want to get out of here.'

'No problem. Do you want me to come and get you?'

I don't want to make Jackie drive all this way. And anyway, I need some space to clear my head. 'No, I'm alright. I'll get the train.'

'Are you okay finding the right one?'

'Yep. It'll be from Paddington, right?'

As I stand on the tube into the city, leaning on the pole, I think about what I gave up for this. A road trip with my friends. And for what? The fantasy of some half-decent grandparents. Sasha and Nell will be having an amazing time. I miss them so much. I wish I'd gone with them instead of staying for this. I finally scroll through their messages, starting with last night's, and the photos of the campsite and sunset.

Hetal messaged early this morning.

Then her messages switch to all caps. What? She's not going with her family? She's going to catch up with the others? My heart fills. I'm so pleased for her. Hetal especially was so desperate for us all to be together. But I can't stop that stab of pain. I'm missing out. What I wouldn't give to be with them. I've thrown away going with them for grandparents who don't want me and I wish I could wind back time and pick again. I'd pick them.

I can't read any more. I made my choice. Got to live with it now.

There's not a train back to Totnes for ages, so I wander aimlessly about London, finally getting to Paddington station a few hours later. It's packed with people, all knowing where they're going, all walking fast. I stand under the big display and scan for my train. There's one in twenty minutes and the platform is up already. I turn to go to the train and freeze. It can't be. It *can't* be.

'Hetal!' I shout across the busy station. 'HETAL!'

She turns my way and grins. 'Cam!'

I run to her and hug her tight. It is so good to see her.

'Wow! What are the chances?' I can't get my head around the fact she's here.

'Actually, the odds are pretty high. I was just about to call you.'

'What?'

'I take it you haven't read your messages?'

'No! What? Why?'

'Jackie rang me. She was worried about you and wondered if I'd heard from you. I said I hadn't and told her I was on my way to catch up with the others.'

Jackie rang Hetal?

'Anyway, we cooked up a plan that I'd meet you here and we could travel together to catch up with Sasha and Nell. If you want to. Though please say yes. It won't be the same without you.'

'But…' My brain is scrambled.

'She even dropped off your passport,' she says, waggling it in front of my face.

Jackie is all kinds of awesome.

I hug Hetal again and this time the tears are happy ones.

CHAPTER 9
SASHA

Tuesday

I chat to the woman about her dog, whose name is Hugo, as Nell sits on the wall and drips. The woman's very sorry he's been so naughty. I get the feeling this isn't the first time he's been in trouble. Hugo however doesn't look remotely sorry, tongue hanging out and grinning.

Nell isn't hurt. Just soaked to the skin. Though her phone doesn't work. She's muttering about getting some rice to put it in, to see if that helps. If you could bring a phone back to life by staring at it, Nell would have managed it, but I'm not sure there's much you can do for it once it's been full-on drowned in a fountain.

I tickle Hugo's ears and he licks my hand, before he gets led away, still being gently scolded in French.

'What a daft hound,' I say to Nell.

She looks up from her phone. 'Yeah. Totally daft.'

'Want to go back and get changed?'

Nell nods. She gets up, leaving a puddle where she's been sitting. I try to suppress a giggle. As she walks, each footstep is a squelch, and I can't contain it.

'You know, that was very funny.'

Nell manages a smile. 'I can imagine it looked that way.'

'No need to imagine,' I say passing her my phone. 'I got the whole thing. Look I can make you fall in on repeat.'

'Oh, great!'

'It's the way your feet flip backwards. The angle. Just hilarious.' I can't stop laughing. Hugo's charging around in the video, woofing, clearly delighted at the commotion he's caused.

I play it again. Everything about it is hilarious. Nell's not laughing though. In fact, she's not even listening anymore.

'Are you sure you didn't hurt yourself?' Perhaps I've misread her reactions.

'No, I'm fine. It's just my phone. I need it to

work.' She's back to staring at it again and jabbing the screen. 'Oh, COME ON!' She gives it a shake in frustration.

'Let me find out what to do with a wet phone.' I search on my phone for advice. 'It says somewhere warm and dry, and fingers crossed, it might start working again. In a few days.'

'A few days? I can't wait a few days. What about rice? Rice might be quicker.'

I scroll down. 'No. Still a few days. And it looks like some people say rice is a bad idea. Something about getting rice in your ports.'

Nell smiles weakly. 'And no one wants rice in their ports.'

It's good to see her smile. 'Come on. Let's get back to the campsite. You can change and I'll see what we can do to save your phone. And in the meantime, you can always use mine.'

'Thanks. I need to let Mum know. You know what she's like. She'll freak out if she can't get in contact with me.'

'I'm guessing not being able to message Tom is the real kicker though, right?' I say gently.

She nods. 'It was going so well. I just really like him, you know? I've fancied him for so long and we've finally got together and it's good.'

I get it. I remember that buzz of excitement when I was with Pierre last summer. As it turned out he was a lying, two-timing scumbag, but the time we spent together was like being drunk on love.

'Borrow my phone and message him now.' I think for a second. 'And now Hetal's coming, you don't have to stay. I mean, if you don't want to. Mum only said I had to have one friend with me…'

I don't want her to go home. But I don't want her to feel sad either.

'Don't be daft!' she says. 'I've fancied Tom for months, but I've literally been dreaming of this sort of freedom for years. A road trip with my best mates? There's nowhere I'd rather be.'

As Nell's getting changed and texting her mum and Tom, I put her phone on the dashboard of the car. It's due to be in the thirties for the next few days. If that doesn't warm it up and dry it out, I don't know what will. Nell comes out of her pod, a bundle of wet clothes in her arms, and hands me back my phone.

'Thanks very much,' she says. 'Mum says she'll post a cheap replacement phone to the wedding venue. I just have to let her know the address.'

'No worries, I'll send her the invitation, it'll be on that,' I say as my phone rings. 'Ooooh, I bet it's

Tom. Don't worry. I'll tell him you can't get to the phone right now. Too many interesting French boys to see.'

'Don't you dare,' she says trying now to snatch the phone back off me, but I hold it out of reach, still ringing.

I laugh. 'Just kidding; it's only Hetal.'

'What do you mean, it's only Hetal?' says Hetal from the phone.

We both laugh. 'Nothing,' I say.

'How's the planning going?' says Nell.

'Great!' She turns her phone so we can see that she's on the train. 'Managed to get the Eurostar fine. And look who I bumped into.'

She pans her phone round to show…

'CAM!' Nell and I scream together.

'What the hell's she doing with you?' I ask.

'Er, rude,' says Cam, a smile in her voice.

'I thought you were seeing your grandparents,' says Nell.

'I was,' she says.

We pause, expecting her to explain but she doesn't.

'So does this mean, we're all going to be together?' I say. 'That makes it a bona fide road trip!'

'It does,' says Hetal, beaming.

'You'd better clear the tent and make room for us,' says Cam.

Nell and I exchange looks: our things have completely engulfed every square inch of the tent. There's stuff even spilling out of the doorway.

'Not a problem,' says Nell. 'When does your train get in?'

'Not for hours yet,' says Cam.

'About five,' says Hetal, checking a timetable.

'Brilliant!' I say. 'We can do something fun this evening to celebrate.'

'I can't believe they're coming,' I say to Nell after we hang up. 'We're getting a whole road trip all together!'

Nell's grinning back. 'All of us together. It's going to be perfect! But you know what isn't perfect? This tent! It's a bombsite. I'm not sure they'll be able to get in, let alone have space for their stuff.'

As I shove clothes to the edges of our tent, my wedding shoes fall out of a bag. I think about Dad. And his wedding. Am I doing the right thing? The right thing isn't always the easy thing Mum says, and the easiest thing in the world would be not to go. His words echo: unreliable, selfish, always causing trouble. Perhaps me turning up unannounced is me causing trouble again?

I sigh.

If I let him know I'm going in advance, I'll have to be a bridesmaid again. And there's not a chance I'm wearing that dress. Wedding crashing it is.

On the upside, Hetal and Cam will be here soon so however the wedding turns out, at least we get to go on a road trip all together.

CHAPTER 10
HETAL

Tuesday

I pretend I'm looking out at the countryside flying past the train window, but really I'm looking at Cam in the reflection. She's not said anything about what happened at her grandparents'. Jackie didn't seem to know much either.

'Have a smashing time,' she'd said. 'And give Cam an extra big hug from me. Tell her to call me if she gets a chance.'

'Is everything okay?' I'd asked Jackie.

'Phil didn't know exactly what happened, and Cam hasn't said, but I'm sure she'll tell you all about it when she's ready.'

But Cam hasn't told me all about it. She's only

said it didn't work out. Her phone buzzes on the table in front of her but she ignores it.

I raise my eyebrows. 'You going to get that?' Is it just me, or shouldn't you always answer the phone. Or at least check who it is.

Cam rolls her eyes but picks up her phone and checks the screen. 'Unknown caller.' She clears her throat, cancels the call and puts her phone back on the table.

I've known Cam a really long time. I know when she's lying. She knows who's trying to call her, so why doesn't she answer? I bet it's got something to do with what's gone on at her grandparents.

'Oh, I nearly forgot, Jackie said if you get a minute could you give her a ring.'

Cam nods. 'No problem. I'll ring her later.'

I frown. What is going on with her? It's not like her to lie. She's usually heart-on-her-sleeve, tell-you-straight Cam. What's happened that's so bad she can't even tell me? Or perhaps our friendship isn't as strong as it used to be. It's a good thing we're getting to go on this road trip. We've got loads of time to reconnect.

Whatever it is, she doesn't want to talk about it, so I dig through my bag and bring out the duplicate itinerary folder I made so I could follow Sasha and Nell's trip.

'What's that?' asks Cam, sitting up a bit and leaning forward.

'I did a little planning.'

'A little? Holy camel. You've got enough there to organise a full-on state visit. Okay then, pitch me the highlights of the trip. What have we got to look forward to?'

'Well, first of all, thank you for choosing to travel with Hetal Holidays, here for all your holidaying needs.' I put on a voice, and Cam grins.

'Seriously, who else would I travel with?'

'First stop will be the historic town of Saint Malo, with a stunning old town, gorgeous boutiques and eateries and a beautiful seaport.'

'Sounds … great,' she says.

I frown. Of course it sounds great. But there's a fleck of sarcasm to her voice.

'What's not to love?'

'Don't get me wrong. Sounds perfect if you're like forty or something. Really safe. Just wondered if there was anything a bit more, well, fun? A bit adventurous maybe.'

'You can walk round the old town walls?'

Cam snorts. 'I can't wait for the adrenaline rush.'

Oh no. I've got this whole holiday all wrong. I thought everyone would want chilled and interesting with sprinklings of food and history and gorgeous views.

I stop talking about the plans, quietly close the folder and pick up my phone. Cam's already distracted by something out of the window, so doesn't notice that I'm now frantically Googling high-adrenaline sports on our route. Just thinking about throwing myself off something only attached to a bungee rope makes me feel ill. White water rafting looks marginally better but is so expensive. At least a good view is usually free.

'I'm going to see if there's anything worth eating in the buffet car,' says Cam, standing up and stretching. 'Want anything?'

'No, thanks,' I say.

I watch her as she walks away, swaying slightly with the rhythm of the train.

I'm sure this holiday will be fine. More than fine. I flick open the folder again and go through the places and activities and restaurants and cafés and campsites. They're all the best I could find. This holiday is a gift. Who knows when we'll get to do something like this again, if ever. Next year everyone will be going different ways, have different plans. This is our last chance at a perfect summer, and I want it to be just that. Perfect.

Cam comes back and we both sleep a bit. Being up till three this morning feels like days ago and I'm starting to feel like the living dead. We change in Paris, grateful that the walk between trains isn't too long and our bags aren't too heavy. Then it's a couple of hours to Saint Malo.

We pull into the station, and jump down off the train, checking we've got all our stuff. Sasha and Nell should be waiting for us. I look along the platform but they're not here. We leave the station and check up and down the road outside. No sign of Sasha's car. No sign of Sasha or Nell.

I check my phone for messages, but there's nothing. I send a quick one.

Hey guys, we're here!! Where are you???

Sasha's read and replying.

So sorry. We've broken down but we're not too far away (I think). I'll send you our location and you can walk to meet us. Then we can all be broken down together!

'You seen this?' I ask Cam, holding up my phone.

She reads then snorts. 'Come on, then; which way is it? Let's go and see if we can figure out what's wrong with the car.'

I work out the way to them, but I'm panicking. I don't know anything about cars, or why they break down or how to fix them. This is not the perfect way to start a perfect road trip.

Cam elbows me gently. 'Cheer up. It's only the car that's broken.'

'But this is a road trip. In a car!'

'I know, that's what makes it so funny.' She laughs.

How does she manage to do that? I don't want to ruin things so I manage a weak smile. I'm sure there are garages in the area, people who can fix cars. And Sasha's French is brilliant. It'll be fine.

I repeat it a couple more times, just to make sure:

It'll be fine. It'll be fine.

CHAPTER 11
NELL

Tuesday

The cars whoosh past us as we sit on the grass verge. Sasha's tried and tried to get the engine to start but it only splutters. It's going nowhere. Now's not the time to ask, but all I want to know is, has Tom replied? Has he got my message about my phone breaking? Or has he ignored the message because it's from a number he didn't recognise?

Sasha's on the phone to her mum, who, all credit to her, isn't panicking. Unlike me who's basically a bag of skin holding only crackling nerves.

'Are there any warning lights?' Sasha's mum says. 'Is the engine too hot? Does it need oil?'

Sasha looks more closely at the dashboard.

'There's only one warning light, but it can't be that. We shouldn't need fuel yet.'

I imagine Sasha's mum face palming.

'Well, clearly you do! At least we know it's nothing serious,' she says. 'Find a petrol station and bring back some fuel. You'll have to buy a petrol can.'

'Okay,' says Sasha. She's struggling not to laugh. 'Thanks, Mum.'

She hangs up and laughs loudly. 'I can't believe that! I was sure we had loads left.'

'But hasn't the warning light been on?' I ask.

'Yes, but Hetal's plan said we'd have enough to last us until at least the next stop. We haven't done loads of extra miles, have we?'

I frown. It's not like Hetal to get things wrong.

'Did I hear my name?'

We both whip round and a little way down the road are Cam and Hetal, laden down with bags and looking like the best thing I've ever seen.

'You found us!' shrieks Sasha, running along the side of the road towards them.

I run after her and we smoosh into a big group hug.

'So, what's the problem?' asks Hetal, nodding towards the car, hazard lights blinking.

'Out of fuel.'

Hetal frowns. 'You should have loads left. Perhaps you've got a leak. A full tank should have got you halfway down France.'

Sasha tilts her head. 'A full tank?'

'Yes, you always start a journey with a full tank.'

'Ah,' said Sasha. 'That might be the problem.'

Cam is laughing hard.

Hetal's distraught. 'I'm so sorry. I just assumed. I should have put that on the list of things to do before you left.'

'No worries. Just goes to show how much I trust you,' says Sasha, nudging Hetal gently. 'I even ignored the warning light because you would know better.'

Cam's pretty much crying.

We're stood right on the edge of the road. I don't like the way lorries are rattling past us. If I had my phone, I'd Google where the nearest petrol station is. 'So shall we get some fuel then?'

Hetal has the details in a flash. 'The closest is less than a mile away, straight down this road.'

'That's lucky,' I say.

'I'll go,' says Sasha. 'Do some of us need to stay with the car?'

'I'll come with you,' says Cam, jumping up. 'I've

been sat down way too long today. You guys stay with the car. We'll be back in no time.'

'Sasha? Can I borrow your phone while you're gone?'

'Sure.' She throws it over to me and I catch it.

'Thanks.'

Cam sets off, stopping to throw her big bag onto the back seat of the car on her way past and Sasha hurries to catch her up.

'How was the journey?' I say to Hetal who is checking for the best place to sit on the verge.

'Long, but totally worth it.' She grins.

I'm about to ask her if she knows how it went with Cam's grandparents, when she cuts in first.

'What's the campsite like? What have you done today? I want to hear about everything I've missed.'

'You missed pancakes on the beach.'

'What?! How can you have done that without us?'

I grin. 'Like you'd do anything different.'

Hetal starts checking out things on her phone, so I get out Sasha's phone. My mum's replied saying she's got a new phone sorted and sent to the wedding venue, and she hopes I can get my clothes dry. I look up at the road with the heat coming off it in waves and grin. Not going to be a problem.

But there's still no reply from Tom. I log into Instagram on my account. I should be able to contact Tom through this. Does he check Instagram? It's worth a shot. I scan down my feed first, seeing what everyone else is getting up to in the first week of the holidays. Loads of beach shots; Yasmin's got a new puppy. I'm so here for puppy content.

Then a photo comes up that makes my skin prickle. It's of someone stood in front of Wendy's deli. And that someone is Ariel. Tom's ex, Ariel. I quickly read the caption.

Look who's landed a job at the gorgeous deli in town! Score! And you'll never guess who I'm working with every day? None other than the gorgeous @Tom_987! Double score. Who knows ... perhaps something will happen over the pork pies and cream buns ☺

I read it again, hoping I've somehow got it wrong. Ariel's working at the deli? She's my replacement? Tom didn't mention *that* in his message.

I look further down and see that Tom's commented.

Looking forward to working with you @Ariel.Daviessss.

I feel numb. How can he say that? And what does it mean? Is he just being polite, or is he really looking forward to working with her?

I click off Sasha's phone, pull my knees up to my chest and hug them to me, wishing with all my heart I was back home so I could talk to Tom.

I call him. I let it ring but he doesn't pick up.

Perhaps that's my answer.

Sasha and Cam come back from the petrol station laughing and chatting.

'You were quick,' says Hetal.

'We don't mess about,' says Cam. 'Now let's get this car going. I'm dying to crash out.'

Sasha fills up the tank, with Hetal giving instructions on the importance of not spilling a flammable liquid and not smoking near an open tank.

'None of us smoke,' Cam says.

Hetal raises her eyebrows. 'You can't be too careful.'

Sasha jumps into the driver's seat and tries the engine. It starts first time, purring into life.

'Yesss!' says Cam, punching the air.

'Have we got everything?' says Hetal, checking where we were sitting.

We cram into the car. I'm in the back with Cam, Hetal's in the passenger seat. It's an unspoken fact that Hetal's going to be the best navigator. They're all chatting but I'm not listening. All I can think about is Tom and Ariel. I think about what Sasha said, about me going home. And that's totally possible now she's got Hetal *and* Cam. But then I look at Sasha, hair thrown back, sunglasses on, laughing at something Hetal's explaining. Hetal's deep into commentary on the history of the road we're travelling along. Cam rolls her eyes at me, but she's grinning. The windows are down, the music is up and I know for sure, there's nowhere I'd rather be. These girls are my life.

Sasha pulls the car slowly up next to our tent. The weather must have been dry for weeks as the whole field is crispy and brown.

'Welcome,' she says, flourishing her hand towards the large tent. We'd given it our best shot but even so, some of the guy ropes look less than perfect and the whole tent is slightly off centre. Still, it's not fallen down yet.

We get out of the car, Hetal and Cam get their bags and go to find which pods are theirs. We'll have a bit of time before we do anything else.

'Sasha?' I ask. 'Could I borrow your phone for a bit? Just want to try and get another message to Tom.'

'No worries.' She hands it over before going into the tent to chat to the others.

I check the message I sent to Tom. Still no reply. He's not even read it. I hit the call button again. He should be out of the deli by now. It rings. And rings. No answer and it clicks through to the automated voice message. I hang up.

I'm trying not to think it but my brain floods with panic. He's ignored my messages. He's ignored my calls. I bet it's because he's out with Ariel. I can't help but go to Instagram.

Ariel's account has a new post. It's her and Tom, smiling together behind the counter in the deli, snapped off baguettes in their hands.

First day done and loving the singing clean-up with wonder-woman Wendy. This deli has the best co-workers. Can't wait to spend the summer with him.

Can't wait to spend the summer *with him*. Not *them. Him.*

I try calling Tom again.

CHAPTER 12
CAM

Tuesday

The view over the sea from our tent as the sun is setting is dramatic enough for me to ignore my phone easily. It's been ringing on and off all afternoon. I've told Jackie I'm fine, but I'm not sure she believes me. She knows me well enough to know that I can't be pushed into sharing. Phil on the other hand hasn't stopped calling and messaging. Thing is, I don't know what to say to him. Your mother's evil? And what if he takes her side? Then what? I can't even deal with that thought so I've put my phone on silent and tucked it into the bottom of my bag and that's where it's going to stay. I'm here, in this awesome place, with my awesome friends on an awesome road trip and I will not let my family dramas spoil this.

Hetal's got the barbeque going and has laid out some sausages on the grill. It smells amazing.

'Another few minutes and we can eat,' she calls.

We've chilled out here since we got back, chatting, playing card games and watching the other people on the campsite. Sasha's shown us the video of Nell falling into the fountain. It's absolutely hilarious. I can't believe Sasha managed to get it! The flip as her feet go up in the air, the almost comic-like splash. Classic.

'Okay, food's up,' calls Hetal.

We grab the rest of the food and the drinks and set up around the barbeque, the smoke making everyone on the campsite jealous.

The first bite is always the best. That combination of juicy and charcoal is just to die for.

'Mmmmm,' says Sasha, articulating what we're all thinking.

'Seconded,' says Nell through a mouthful. 'This is amazing, Hetal.'

Hetal's beaming. 'I knew this would be the perfect spot for a barbeque. That view.'

We all look out over the sea, which is

unbelievably still, the sun turning it dark blue against the pink of the sky.

'You've planned it all brilliantly,' I say. 'You've thought of everything.'

'I still can't believe we're all here,' says Sasha. 'On Saturday, this wasn't even a plan! And we haven't been all together in ages and now we're going to have nearly two whole weeks. I feel like there's loads I need to catch up on. Like what is going on with everyone?'

We look round at each other. Sasha's right. Other than Saturday, we haven't all been together in a really long time. Have we fallen out of the habit? Life's been so busy though. I've been working, Nell too, and Hetal's spent every moment studying. Or is it that we haven't really made the effort?

'How did it go with your grandparents, Cam?' asks Sasha.

I notice Hetal and Nell exchange looks. I feel sick.

'Oh fine. No drama. Just realised I'd prefer to be with you guys.' I smile, trying to convince them, or me, or both.

Sasha raises her eyebrows but says nothing.

'I want to hear everything about Tom,' says

Hetal, changing the subject. 'That's all going well, right?'

Nell looks worried. 'I think so? Honestly, I don't know what to think.'

'It seemed all on from where I was standing when you left yesterday.'

Nell blushes. 'That was then.'

'What's changed?' I ask.

'Okay. Right. I need to get your opinion. Because I don't know. I left and everything was fine. Lots of messages, he's missing me, nice stuff. Then he sent a message saying there was someone temporarily standing in for me at the deli.'

'I saw that one,' says Sasha. 'Not in a weird creepy way,' she says to me and Hetal. 'It pinged up as we were looking at photos.'

'Then I got knocked into the fountain and my phone died. I wasn't really worried about that, more that my phone was dead so I couldn't keep in touch with him. But then I looked on Instagram and you'll never guess who the temporary stand-in is.'

'Who?' asks Hetal.

'Ariel.'

'What?!' says Sasha. 'Tom's ex, Ariel?'

'Yep.'

'Craaappp,' I say. Then instantly regret it when I see Nell's face.

'See? I knew I wasn't being paranoid. That's not good, is it? They'll get back together; I'll get dumped and maybe even lose my job.'

'It may not be as bad as it looks,' I say.

'Sasha, can I borrow your phone?' Nell opens Ariel's Instagram and passes it round.

It does look bad. Ariel definitely wants to get back with Tom.

'It doesn't mean *he'll* want to,' says Hetal, but her voice isn't certain. 'Though I'm not the best expert on things of the heart.'

Not an expert? Hetal and Finn have been together for nearly a year. That's expert in my books.

'So,' says Sasha, looking at Nell, 'what are you going to do about it? Did you message Tom about your phone?'

'Yes. And I tried ringing him. But he didn't answer.'

We're all quiet. I'll be honest, it doesn't sound great.

'That's not good, is it? I don't know what else I can do, all the way over here.'

'Perhaps it's for the best,' says Sasha.

Nell's head whips round. 'For the best? How can this be considered *best* in any way?'

'I'm with Nell. How's that a good thing?' I say.

For a moment it looks like Sasha's going to back out of what she's about to say. 'Last summer, I didn't tell you, I met a boy. He was wonderful.'

'Three questions,' says Hetal, interrupting. 'How did you meet? What was his name? Why didn't you tell us?'

Sasha laughs. 'He was a waiter at the local restaurant. I know. Total cliché. His name was Pierre, and I didn't tell you because I was embarrassed.'

Sasha? Embarrassed? That's not like her. She's super-confident. Always sure of herself. Knows exactly what she's doing.

Sasha sighs. 'He was perfect. We had an amazing couple of weeks. One evening I couldn't meet up with him. But then my plans changed, so I went to find him.'

We're all hanging on her every word.

'Let's just say, he'd made other plans. With someone else. I was so angry with myself for having fallen for him, for letting my guard down. But,' she turns to Nell, 'I was glad I found out what he was like before it went on too long. As amazing as it was, it was just an illusion. It wasn't real.'

'But Tom's not like that!'

'In which case he won't be bothered by Ariel working with him. And if he is like Pierre, you'll find out before you're too invested.'

Nell's chewing her lip. 'I guess you're right. If he can't last two weeks without me, there's no hope.'

'And if he is as lovely as you say he is, then this won't even vaguely be a problem.'

Sasha's right. And I hope for Nell's sake it works out.

'I'm sorry you didn't feel like you could tell us about Pierre,' says Hetal.

'Yeah,' I say. 'We could have made a Pierre doll and stuck pins in him.'

Sasha laughs. 'That would have been good. But it's not a problem. I've moved on.'

I grin. 'Anytime you change your mind, we're totally here for you. And how about you Hetal? Everything peachy on Finn love island?'

Hetal's face changes. 'Ha. Finn.' She fiddles with a strand of hair. 'We're not so much together anymore.'

'What? No!' I say. 'When did *that* happen? Why am I always so behind on all the goss?'

'You're not behind. It only happened on Thursday. And I've not really told anyone. It's no biggie. And not really a massive surprise. It was always going to be hard making it work long distance.'

She doesn't look like it's no biggie but none of us push her.

'Anytime you want us to work any voodoo karma retaliation on Finn, you just say, okay?' I smile at her.

Hetal doesn't smile back. 'No, it's okay, thanks. I think I was the bad guy in that relationship.'

Sasha's frowning. 'I can't believe that. You'd never do anything to hurt someone.'

Hetal shrugs. 'I didn't mean to. I think I got too busy and kind of forgot that we were supposed to be together. There seemed to be so many things that were more important, more urgent.' She picks at the grass beside her. 'I don't blame him for ending it. But I am sad it ended like that.'

Everyone's been carrying so much emotional stuff – Sasha and the guy from last summer, Nell and her worries about Tom, and Hetal with her breakup. They don't need my family drama added to this. I'm definitely keeping that to myself.

There's a noise from behind the tent next to ours. A mother cat is walking along the row of tents, a trail of five kittens behind her which is causing a chorus of 'ahhhhs' to follow them.

'Ah, they're so sweet,' says Sasha. 'Come on, come on. Here puss puss.' She dangles a long piece of grass playfully.

We soon have a collection of cats mewing around us, tripping over our feet and putting their heads into our cups to sip our drinks. One little tortoiseshell kitten comes right up to me and clambers onto my lap and starts to claw her way up my t-shirt.

'Hey, little one,' I say, tickling her ears. She might actually be the cutest thing I've ever seen.

The mother cat and the other kittens start walking off. I lift her down off me. 'Hurry up. You don't want to be left behind.' But it takes quite a few attempts before she realises the rest of her family have left without her and she scampers after them.

It's been pretty much a perfect evening.

That is until about three-thirty the next morning, when things start to feel not so perfect.

CHAPTER 13
SASHA

3.30 a.m. Wednesday

I'm awake with the weirdest feeling. I can't work out what it is. Is it wedding worries? Has the thought of that awful dress and whether I have to wear it woken me up? I glance at my phone. It's the middle of the night and inside the tent it's pitch black and silent.

I feel sick.

Very sick.

Like I'm going to be sick.

I'm going to be sick.

I push back my covers and fumble with the zip on my pod. I *cannot* be sick in the tent. We'd never get rid of the smell. I crawl across the living space and throw myself out of the front of the tent. I need to get to the toilet block *now*.

I stumble about, trying to figure out which way it is. The moon's full, so I'm able to pick out the shadows of tents and trailers. At least I can avoid being sick on them.

I suddenly figure out where I am and run towards the toilets. I push open the door, the bright fluorescent lights temporarily blinding me. I stagger into a stall and throw up. I'm hoping my aim is good because my eyes are tight shut.

After I've finished, I wipe my mouth, flush the toilet, and walk out of the cubicle to wash my hands. Cam is leaning against the wall, her hair tied messily back, looking like I feel.

'You too, huh?' she says. 'I did wonder if I'd see anyone else in here.'

'What? You're sick as well? Eugh. I feel so crap.' My mouth feels like things have died in it.

'Must be a bug or something. Hope the other two are okay. I guess we'll find out.'

We go outside and sit, leaning against the toilet block as the fresh air is better than the stinking humidity inside. Like Cam says, it smells like someone's thrown up in there.

We take it in turns to run back in as the sickness

comes in waves. We're both outside again when we see a figure stumbling in the darkness.

'Odds on that's Hetal or Nell,' whispers Cam in the darkness next to me.

'I really hope not.'

But it is. Nell comes staggering up to the block, clatters open the door and disappears inside. The noises confirm that she's offloading her tea. After a few minutes, it's all gone quiet.

'I'll go and see how she's doing,' I say and stand up, my legs feeling shaky and unsteady.

Nell's leaning against the wall, splashing water on her face.

'Hey,' I say.

She jumps. 'What are you doing here? Did I wake you? I'm sorry – I tried so hard to sneak out quietly.'

'Nah, you didn't wake me. Cam and I were already here.'

Nell groans. 'You guys are sick too?'

I nod. 'We're just taking a break from it outside though.'

'Hope Hetal's okay,' says Nell.

We step out into the fresh air. Cam seems to have dropped off to sleep sitting up. We sit a little further away, so we don't disturb her.

'Not exactly the road trip we imagined,' I say.

The ultimate in irony if I'm too sick to get to the wedding.

Nell chuckles. 'I bet it'll just be a twenty-four-hour thing. You watch. This won't spoil it.' She pauses. 'Oh, hold on. Got to go.' She jumps up and runs back into the toilet block.

I like that she's trying to be upbeat, but I can't help feeling a bit rubbish about everything. Then I imagine my mum saying, 'Everything's always worse at night. Wait till the morning. It all feels better in the morning.'

I hope that's true because right now I just want to be at home with my mum and in my own bed.

Nell comes out. 'Not sure there's anything left inside me.'

'Thanks for the overshare.'

'No problem.' She sits down. 'I bet we'll look back on this and laugh.'

'Yeah, probably. Might take me a few years though.'

'I want to say thank you for what you said this evening.'

'About what?'

'About Pierre and what happened last summer. You didn't have to share that, but it was helpful to hear.'

'No worries. And thanks for being the one who made this trip possible – without you I wouldn't have been allowed to come on my own. So don't forget, because of me you're now in a French field, barfing into a Portaloo.'

Nell laughs. 'Who would want to miss out on All This Fun?'

'In which case, you're welcome!' I say and grin.

'I think I need to go to bed,' she says. 'How about we wake up Cam and go back to the tent?'

I yawn. 'Sounds like a plan.'

We nudge Cam awake and link arms with her before walking back to the tent.

'Night,' I whisper to them as we crawl into our separate pods. 'Hope you get some sleep.'

'You too,' Nell says. Cam's already face-planted onto her bed.

I crawl under my covers and pass out.

I wake to the sound of Hetal humming outside the tent. My insides feel hollow and my limbs like they're solid stone. At least I didn't have to get up again last night. I wonder how the others are. From the sound of it, Hetal didn't get sick.

I unzip my pod and lean out. Hetal pops her head through the tent flap.

'Morning! Fancy some breakfast? I've been out and got some fresh croissants.'

Bleurgh. 'I'm not sure I can.'

'What's wrong?' Her face is creased with worry.

'I was really sick in the night. We all were.'

'All were?'

'Yeah. Cam first, then me, then Nell. Must be some sort of bug. Or something we ate. Though it can't be, because we all ate the same things.'

Hetal's really looking concerned now. 'You think it could be something you ate? It wouldn't be the barbeque, would it?'

'But you ate it too.'

Hetal looks gutted. 'Actually, I didn't. Once I'd cooked it, I didn't fancy it, so I just had a salad roll.'

I groan and rest my head on the floor.

'I'm so sorry,' says Hetal. 'I didn't know. I can't have cooked it properly.'

'It doesn't matter. We've survived the night, so it's all good. Are the others up yet?'

'No, not yet. I did think it was strange no one else was up. Are you able to drive?'

'I'm sure I'll be okay. Just give me a few more minutes,' I say. Or a few more hours, maybe.

'You look pale. It's not like just driving down the road to the shops; the next section of our journey is nearly five hours. We don't want to set off, not make it and then not have a plan for where to camp. We could stay here another day – set off tomorrow instead. I'll look again at the journey and see if we can squeeze it into the time we'll have left.'

'There's no way we can stay another day,' comes Cam's sleepy voice from the next pod. 'The toilets smell rank.'

'That sounds great,' I say to Hetal, as I retreat back into my pod. 'Tomorrow would be better.'

I can't believe she didn't cook the sausages properly. Everyone knows that about barbeques surely. And now we've lost a whole day because of it. Do we have enough time still to get to the wedding? I don't even know. But right now, I feel so awful I'm not sure I care.

It's at least six hours since I last moved, but I'm starting to feel like I need some fresh air. And possibly some food. Nothing barbequed. Obviously. Never having barbequed anything ever again.

I can hear Cam and Nell are up too.

'Hey,' says Hetal. 'You're awake. We were just thinking about going down to the beach. Want to come?'

'Sounds good.'

By the time I've eaten something, changed my clothes and had a cool drink of water, I'm feeling more human. We wander down the path leading to the beach, Hetal busy reading us facts about the coastline, wildlife we might see, World War Two history of the area ... I let the words wash over me.

The sun's dipping in the sky and everything has a pinky, golden hue. We walk down onto the sand, then along the seashore, tiny, frothy waves lapping our feet.

'Who's for a swim?' says Cam.

'But our swimming costumes are back at the campsite. And we don't have towels,' says Hetal, always the voice of reason.

'So what?' says Cam. She's stripping down to her underwear – a cropped bra top and boxers. 'Who's coming?'

She throws her clothes up the beach, turns and strides into the sea. 'Oh frick – it's so cold!'

'You're not being very convincing, you know,' Nell calls after her.

Cam is nearly waist-deep now, and dives in, shooting back up, water slicking her pink hair to her head. 'Come on! You'll regret it if you don't!'

Her words are the trigger we need. Nell plunges straight in, fully dressed, screaming the whole way. I stop long enough to take off my clothes and shoes, and tuck my phone inside them before running after Nell.

The coldness of the water bites at my skin as I wade deeper. I mustn't stop. If I stop I'll never get all the way in. With a shriek, I dunk my head under the water. My whole body feels alive, my skin crackling with the stinging cold. 'Oh, that's good!' I gasp.

Hetal's the last in, mainly because she's been gathering everyone's scattered clothes and taking them higher up the beach.

'Hetal! Hetal! Hetal!' the three of us chant from the sea.

'I'm going to drag you in,' shouts Cam.

Hetal can't fight the inevitable, and she's stripped and in and bobbing next to us before Cam can carry out her threat.

'Did you even check to see if this area was a designated swimming section?' she asks.

Cam splashes her. 'Chill out, Hetal. The sea's super calm. There's nothing to worry about.'

Hetal splashes her back, and soon we're all ducking and splashing and laughing and for the next half an hour I forget all about the wedding, and my dad and the pressure not to mess everything up.

CHAPTER 14
HETAL

Thursday

I can't believe my barbeque made everyone sick. How could I have been so stupid? Were the sausages out of date? Or maybe it was just that I didn't cook them properly. I'm sure I did. I should have double-checked. Luckily this morning, everyone's sounding much better. Cam's teasing Nell about her bed hair and Sasha's studying the map to the next campsite.

'I think we should do the next bit of our journey,' Sasha says.

'Are you sure? You've been pretty ill.'

'Totally sure. I feel loads better. Besides, I'm ready for getting stuck into this road trip – the thrill of the open road, the wind in your hair, seeing new places. Let's do it.'

We pack up the car. I go through the order with everyone so that everything fits.

We sit, soaking up the sun and sipping our drinks, overlooking the ocean one last time before we leave. The car doors are open to let in a bit of fresh air before we set off.

'Well, Saint Malo, you've been brilliant,' says Cam, raising her water bottle to the view.

Nell grins. 'I've got strong fountain memories. Cheers, Saint Malo!'

Cam laughs. 'My memories are more toilet-block based.'

'Yeah, hard same,' says Sasha, laughing too.

I know they're only joking, but their words dig into my stomach and make it hurt. It's not been the greatest of starts, running out of fuel, and now this. And both times it was my fault. I try to shake the negative feelings but they're like sticky weed and won't go away.

The next site is good though. I've got to think of it as a fresh start. There's still plenty of time for a great road trip. All I have to do is make sure everything is perfect.

Sasha's phone pings. She checks it and laughs. 'Nell! A message from Tom.'

'Really? Let me see.'

Sasha's laughing. 'Though it's not your Tom. There's a Tom in my French class and he's a bit weirded out by your messages and phone calls.'

'What?' Nell's mouth's hanging open.

'Wrong Tom,' says Cam.

'Ah crap,' says Nell, her head in her hands.

I lean over and hug her. 'It's easily done.'

'But now it's been thirty-six hours without contacting him. He's going to think… I'm not sure what he's going to think, but it's not good.'

'It'll be fine,' I say, more to make Nell feel better rather than knowing it will be *actually* fine.

We finish our drinks and get into the car.

'Next stop, Poitiers,' says Sasha, pulling her seat belt on. 'Cam, you're in charge of the tunes. Hetal, you're navigating. And Nell, do you want my phone so you can actually check in with Tom this time?'

Nell leans forward from the back seat and takes Sasha's phone. 'Thanks, Sasha.'

We pull out of the campsite and onto the road. In my mirror I see Cam lean back on the pillows dangling over from the boot and shut her eyes. Nell's scrolling and tapping away, completely absorbed. And I need to concentrate on getting us there without any dramas.

I scan the route. We're going to go through some amazing scenery.

'How long's it going to take us?' says Sasha, not taking her eyes off the road.

I check my phone. 'It says just over four hours. But I've got some places we can stop, so just say if you need to.'

'Cool,' says Sasha. She drives without speaking for a while. Then says, 'Can I ask you something? You don't really think you were the reason Finn ended it, do you?'

'I don't really know. I didn't exactly call him regularly. But it was always going to be tough. We hardly ever saw each other. I was kind of hoping we'd manage to meet up in the holidays, but I didn't do anything to make that happen. Didn't plan anything, didn't ask Finn if he wanted to. I guess I didn't put much effort in.'

'Isn't it weird that a relationship takes effort, though?' says Sasha. 'I always thought you wouldn't be able to help yourself – you'd want to do all those things and so they'd happen.'

I think for moment. She sort of has a point. 'I guess. In which case, it looks like I didn't really want to meet up or talk to him regularly because I didn't.' I shake my head. 'That's a bit too simplistic though. I think sometimes the things and people right in front of you take up your attention and, this year, that's been my studies. Finn's not been headline news. I can't blame him for not wanting to stick around.'

'Did he organise any meet ups?' Sasha asks.

I frown. 'No.'

Sasha shrugs a bit. 'So maybe it wasn't all your fault after all.'

I know what she's trying to do, she's trying to make me feel better and I love her for it. That's what friends do after all, lift you up. But I know, with Finn, it didn't work because I didn't make it.

Nell hands me Sasha's phone.

'All caught up?'

'Yeah,' says Nell. 'Tom says he won't worry if he doesn't hear from me for a few days. That's not him projecting, is it? That he doesn't actually *want* to hear from me? Or he's going to use it as an excuse not to contact me?'

'No!' says Sasha. 'He's just trying not to put you under pressure to always find a way to message.'

Nell sighs. 'I hope you're right. I said I'd talk to him later once we got to the campsite.'

'Any other Instagrams from Ariel?' I ask.

'A few. The worst one was a shot along the deli counter with Tom at the end.'

'That doesn't sound too bad,' says Sasha.

'The caption was *everything in this deli is delicious*.'

Sasha snorts. 'That's outrageous. I'm sure Tom can see through it. Have you said you know Ariel is working there?'

'I did say I'd spotted it on Instagram.'

'And?' I ask. 'What did he say?'

'He said there was nothing to worry about. She needed a job; the deli needed an extra server. Made sense.'

'Do you think he realises it might make you feel uncomfortable?' Sasha says.

'Not really,' says Nell.

'Perhaps you need to post some pictures of "delicious" French boys and see if he thinks it means something then,' says Sasha.

Cam snorts from the back seat. 'You'd make your point, but you might lose him because of it.'

'Oh, turn this one up,' says Nell.

Feels Like I'm Falling in Love has just started on the playlist and Cam turns it up so it's blaring from the speakers.

Sasha winds her window down and her long hair streams back as she sings. Nell is laughing in the back and Cam is belting out the words. The

French fields fly past as we sing and drive our way down through France, little hamlets coming and going, the open flat countryside gradually being replaced by undulating hills. And finally, I start feeling this road trip could be okay. That it's all going to work out fine. We're finding each other again. Finally, we've got those road trip vibes.

I'm smiling as we pull into the campsite. It looks just like the website – beautiful pitches dotted through a woodland, with a stream. There's a café on site, but I suppose that must be further on.

A man stops us at the gate. '*Avez-vous une reservation?*'

'Yes,' I say, digging through my folder. 'I emailed three days ago to book.'

The man searches down his list, checking our number plate several times. 'I'm sorry. You aren't on my list. And we're fully booked.'

'What?' I say, the panic rising in my throat. 'But I booked.' I open my emails on my phone and scroll. Then I check my junk folder and there it is. The email telling me the campsite hasn't got space. How could I have missed this? I should have checked when I didn't hear back. Tears prick in my eyes, and I can't speak, my throat all tight and scratchy.

'Thank you,' says Sasha, leaning over me. 'Could you tell us if there's another campsite nearby?'

'Of course. There's one in the next town. And they're sure to have space.'

Sasha thanks him again and turns the car round and back onto the road.

Everyone's very quiet.

'I'm so sorry. I thought I'd booked it.' All I seem to be doing this holiday is messing stuff up.

'Don't worry,' says Cam. 'No harm done. And there's a campsite nearby so all good.'

'And you were right,' says Nell, 'it did look amazing.'

'Perhaps we can stay there on our way back,' says Sasha.

I know they're being kind, but it just makes it worse.

Sasha drives to the next town and we follow signs for the campsite, eventually finding it down the end of a dirt track.

I immediately know why the man said they'd definitely have vacancies. It's because no one in their right mind would want to stay in this dump.

CHAPTER 15
NELL

Thursday

The first thing I notice about our unplanned campsite is its complete lack of mobile signal. There's not even a bar showing on Sasha's phone. How can that even be a thing?

'Anyone got signal?' I ask.

Hetal and Cam immediately check their phones.

'No,' says Hetal.

Cam shakes her head.

Hetal looks awful. She seems to be taking this change of plan badly. But why hadn't she checked the reservation? Why did she assume we'd booked? I bet that last campsite had wifi, or at least some signal.

'Ah, never mind,' I say, even though my heart's sinking. I promised Tom I'd call. Sasha said I'd missed a call from him, so when we stopped at the services earlier, I tried to call him back but there was no answer. I just want an actual conversation with him. I wish with every part of me that I had my own phone. That I wouldn't have to rely on having to borrow everyone else's. Bet Tom got fed up of waiting and called Ariel instead. Gah, my brain sometimes. Only three more days until I get my replacement phone.

Hetal seems a bit spaced. We're all sort of waiting for her to say what we do. We've been shown a place where we can camp, and it's not too bad. Just a bit of broken glass to clear before we can put the tent up.

Sasha takes control. 'Okay. Let's clear the pitch, bag up the rubbish first. Then we'll get the tent set up.'

Cam opens the back of the car and shouts. 'Oh my goodness! Look what's in here!'

We run over to her and crowd round. Curled up on top of the jumpers and pillows is the tortoiseshell kitten from the Saint Malo campsite, fast asleep.

'Ahhhh, she's so gorgeous,' I whisper.

'Has she been asleep the whole way, do you think?' says Sasha.

'A cat stowaway!' says Cam, gently stroking her ears with a couple of fingers.

'Technically we've stolen it from the last campsite. They'll be worried sick,' says Hetal. 'We must let them know. How on earth did I not notice? I checked the car before we set off.'

'She must have snuck in,' I say. 'What shall we call her?'

There's a Madonna song playing on Cam's portable speaker.

'How about Madge?' says Cam.

The kitten stirs in her sleep and stretches out.

'She seems to like it,' says Sasha. 'Madge it is.'

'We mustn't lose her,' says Hetal. 'We can take her back to the campsite on our way up to the ferry next week.' She looks at her phone. 'Agh, but I can't let them know because there's no signal.' She throws her phone into the car.

'Try not to let it get to you,' says Sasha. 'We're here, we're all together, having an adventure. We can manage a night without.'

Hetal smiles briefly at Sasha. 'I suppose you're right.'

Not sure who Sasha is kidding.

Sasha and I pick up all the sharp things where we want to put the tent, along with all sorts of random bits of rubbish from the last people who were here. We gather a whole bin bag full. Cam has emptied her bag and has put a scarf in the bottom and gently moved Madge into it. She loops the bag carefully over her head, so her bag is across her body.

'Perfect,' she says. 'Mobile kitten bed.'

Hetal's emptying the car to get to the tent. The pile of things grows bigger as the car empties.

The tent goes up quickly. We've got two more people helping than when Sasha and I put it up and it shows.

Sasha ducks inside and sighs, 'Aah, home,' which makes me laugh. It does weirdly feel like home. We push all our stuff in and fall onto the heap of sleeping bags and pillows and blankets.

'Bliss,' says Sasha. 'Though when I close my eyes, I still feel like I'm in the car.'

'Let's stay at the campsite this evening,' says Hetal. 'I think we're at least two miles from the town, and it'll give you a break from driving.'

'Suits me,' says Sasha, stretching out. 'I'm trashed.'

We eat the food we've got with us, sharing it with Madge as we play card games outside the tent. It's baking hot and doesn't seem to be getting much cooler as the sun gradually sets.

Everyone starts to pack up the stuff and get ready to go to bed.

I borrow Sasha's phone and go to find a decent signal.

'Don't go far,' Hetal calls after me.

I walk off along the track we came along. That way I'll at least know how to find my way back. The crickets in the hedge are deafening and in the twilight I can see bats swooping and diving over my head. I know Hetal doesn't rate this place, and despite the lack of any sort of signal, it's still pretty awesome being all together. I can't believe we're doing this!

I keep checking for a signal as I walk but it stays stubbornly non-existent. I flick the torch on so that I can see where I'm walking. Still no signal. It's now pitch black. We're so far from any big towns or cities that the sky isn't artificially lit and there are so many stars. I spend a few minutes just staring up at them. I don't think I've ever seen so many.

I check the phone one last time. I promised I'd ring but there's not even the tiniest bit of signal. I turn back and walk along the track, a little quicker than I'd walked down it. Darkness does funny things. I keep thinking there's someone behind me. Or there could be someone the other side of the hedge, or a creature hiding in the shadows.

I shine the torch in front of me, using it to scare away the darkness. That's when I come to a fork in the track. I hadn't noticed that before. Which way is it? I swing the torch round to see if there's a sign, but I can't see anything.

I'm just going to have to pick one and hope. I choose the left-hand fork and walk down it for twenty minutes or so. The hedges are a lot higher now, nearly meeting over my head. I don't think this is right. I turn round and go back again, keeping an eye out for the fork so I don't miss it.

The others will be worried. I've been gone for ages now. I get to the fork and go down the right-hand one this time. I recognise a gateway to a field as I pass it and breathe a sigh of relief.

I almost jog the last bit as I'm properly creeping myself out now. I'm even imagining hearing twigs snapping behind me.

I see the tent in the torchlight and hurry to the flap, dragging up the zip.

Someone screams from inside the tent. 'Who's that?'

'It's me! What are you screaming for?'

Sasha grabs me and pulls me inside, quickly zipping up the flap behind me.

'We think we can hear someone,' hisses Hetal, 'walking around our tent.'

I look at their faces, wide-eyed in the torchlight. 'Seriously? Are you sure it wasn't me?'

I'm trying to sound light about it, but the look on their faces tells me they aren't kidding.

'No. We really heard someone,' says Cam.

'Listen,' whispers Sasha.

We all listen, motionless. They're right. There is the sound of footsteps.

'Perhaps it's just some other campers,' I whisper.

'Have you seen anyone else camping here?' asks Hetal.

I haven't.

'I'm never going to be able to sleep with someone out there,' says Hetal.

'How about,' I say, 'we sleep with our pod doors open, and our heads together. That way…' I trail off. I think of all the horror movies I've watched. People always get picked off one by one. At least if we're together, that can't happen.

'Good idea,' says Sasha, shuffling so her legs are inside her pod.

We all settle down, heads together in a semi-circle, listening to the footsteps outside. Cam tucks Madge between us before finding my arm and squeezing it. I reach out my hand to hold Sasha's.

'Good plan,' she whispers, and I hear her reaching for Hetal's hand.

It's silent for a moment, then Cam speaks. 'I know we're all terrified, but anyone else getting strong *Toy Story 3* vibes?'

Which makes us all laugh.

CHAPTER 16
CAM

Friday

Madge is trying to sit on my face. Which is cute until I realise she's a bit stinky. No, it's not her that's stinky, it's the gift she's left me in the bag that stinks.

'Oh, Madge,' I say quietly, tickling her ears, not wanting to wake up the others.

'What is that smell?' says Sasha groggily from her sleeping bag. 'Smells like something's died.'

'Sorry, it's Madge.'

I open the flap to get rid of the cat poo, and right outside, peering down at me is the huge face of a cow. I'm literally nose to snout with it. It sniffs me with its big, black nose.

'Erm, everyone?' I say. 'I think I might have found what we heard last night.'

Everyone looks up and I pull back the flap. The cow sticks its head right into the tent.

Sasha starts laughing, then Nell joins in. What a relief it wasn't someone sneaking around. Hetal's smiling but doesn't quite manage a laugh.

I scratch the nose of the cow who seems more curious than scary and encourage her to move out of the way. Not sure a warm tent is the ideal place to keep a cat poo a second longer.

I push out of the tent, stand up and stretch. There are a dozen cows surrounding our tent and the car. Cool. Cool, cool, cool.

Madge is squirming to get away from me, but I daren't put her down. She'll either run off or get trampled by this dairy herd. I pop her back into the tent and zip it up, hoping that she doesn't disgrace herself again.

As I finish cleaning up the bag, a farmer comes along and herds the cows back into their field, scolding them in French. My French isn't great, but I can pick up that this is a regular thing and he's getting a bit cross about them repeatedly escaping.

'*Bonjour,*' he calls over to me.

I manage a '*Bonjour*' back and feel hugely proud of my clear bilingual abilities.

'*J'espère que mes vaches ne vont pas dérangé hier soir,*' he says.

My moment of pride vanishes. I've not the vaguest idea what he's said. Luckily Sasha sticks her head out of the tent and answers him in fluent French. I now have pride by association. My awesome friend is bilingual. The farmer chuckles and says something else I don't understand, before following the last of his cows out of our field and into theirs.

'What did he say?' I ask.

'He hoped his cows didn't disturb us last night. I said we were terrified, imagining that we were surrounded by axe murderers. He apologised and said at least they didn't trample our tent.'

I laugh. 'Yeah, that would have been terrifying.'

'I'm wondering whether just the one night here might be enough,' says Hetal, joining us, holding Madge in her arms.

'Excellent call,' I say. 'What do you recommend?'

Hetal frowns. It's not like her not to have a plan ready to go.

'The next place planned on the road trip is Saint-Etienne, but that was a longer route to take in some sights. I think the best idea is to take the most direct route and travel as far as we can today. We've lost a day's travelling already. What do you think, Sasha? You up for more driving?'

'Yep! Bring it on!' she says.

'Sounds great,' I say.

We eat some leftover bits of food for breakfast, pack up the tent and set off. The car's hot and sticky so we have the windows down. We decide to stop in Brive-la-Gaillarde. Hetal assures us it's worth stopping there. She keeps saying sorry for things and it's starting to annoy me. We get it. She's made mistakes and she's sorry. Just move on already. It's no big deal. Why can't she just chill?

We get there about lunchtime. Sasha follows signs to the town centre and parks along a tree-lined street. There's hardly anyone about.

Sasha turns off the engine. 'I'm desperate to stretch my legs. I feel like I've been in the car for years.'

We pile out. Madge has slept the whole way, curled up on my lap but now she's wriggling in my arms, desperate to explore.

'I'm going to see if I can find cat food and a lead,' I say. 'Madge is dying to go down.' That and I need some space.

'Good plan,' says Hetal. 'I heard there's a fascinating fifth century church which is open to the public and I would love to see it. And I've Googled pet shops as I thought we might need things for Madge and there's one on the way.'

The idea of an any-century church isn't exactly appealing. Let alone a fifth century one. Definitely a Hetal thing.

'I'm not sure a church is the right place to train a cat on a lead. You go on without me and I'll sort out Madge.'

Sasha and Nell aren't looking pleased with either of those plans. 'You fancy finding some shops?' says Sasha to Nell.

Nell nods. 'You bet. Are you both sure you'll be okay on your own?'

I'm fine with it but not so sure about Hetal. After a moment she says something about being able to really concentrate on all the history. Reckon she's hiding how upset she is that no one else wants to check out the old building with her. She's always so desperate for everyone to be all together and it being perfect. But letting people do what they want and split up for a bit is also fine. Why doesn't she realise that?

'I'll catch up with you both when I've found a

lead. I'll ring and find out where you are. And when you're done, come and find us too, Hetal.'

We split up. Sasha and Nell head towards the shops and Hetal walks off towards the old church. I let out a big whoosh of breath. Finally a bit of space and it's lovely. What happened with Phil's parents must still be getting to me, I usually love being with everyone. I follow Google Maps to the pet shop, which is easy to find and stacked to the ceiling with every type of pet accessory you could ever imagine. And some you'd never imagine! The door dings as I push it open. Instantly I'm reminded of Papa John's hardware shop back home.

The lad behind the counter looks up and says something in French. Why didn't I pay more attention in French classes? He's cute too. Why can't I speak French like Sasha?

'I'm sorry,' I say. 'I don't really speak any French.'

'Ah, you are English?'

'Yes,' I say.

'How can I help?'

'I need a lead, for my cat.' I show him Madge who is now asleep again in my bag.

He comes over and peeps in. 'Ah, so tiny. I have the thing that will work.' He rummages on a shelf and pulls out a harness and lead. 'This is very good. Very, how you say, gentle?'

'Sounds perfect!'

'You want to try it first?'

'That would be useful.'

Together we carefully fit and adjust the harness, so Madge is comfortably in it. He smells good. I look sideways at him and catch him looking at me. He smiles, completely unfazed by getting caught. I smile back, before clipping on the lead.

'Perfect fit!' I say. 'Thank you.' I can feel my cheeks are pink. What's wrong with me? Boys don't usually have this effect on me. He *is* super cute though.

'My pleasure.' Just the way he says *pleasure* makes my face feel hot.

We both go to speak at the same time, then laugh.

'No, you go,' I say.

'I was only saying, I like your hair. Pink, it suits you.'

Which is a good job, as now I'm a beacon of glowing pinkness. 'Thanks,' I say. 'It's not everyone's cup of tea.'

'Cup of tea?' He's looking puzzled.

'Not everyone likes it.' I grin.

'Well, I do.'

I smile. I wish we were staying here longer.

I pay and he's writing something on the receipt.

'Just in case,' he says. 'My number. For if there's a problem with the lead.'

I see he's written his name – Leo – next to his number, all the numbers written slightly differently to at home, with a loopy nine and a flourish on the ones.

'Call me,' he says after I tell him my name.

I leave the shop riding on a wave of hormones – receipt carefully tucked into my wallet, kitten food in a bag and with Madge on her lead. At first, she's not too impressed, thinking it's a toy and turning and biting the lead, but after a few minutes it seems to click and soon she's gambolling along beside me, delighted to be exploring again. We stop and sniff lots of things, but it's too hot to rush, so I let her lead me.

The street opens into a square, with trees and benches and we set off across it in search of Sasha and Nell. I feel my phone buzz in my pocket. I'll just see who that is.

It's Phil. It's been three days since I left, and I've not spoken to him since. I don't know what to say, but perhaps I should just say that.

'Hello?'

'Cam? Thank goodness! Are you okay?'

'Yes. I'm fine.' Apart from the trauma of meeting your parents, I don't add.

'I owe you an apology.'

What? It's not Phil who needs to apologise. It should be his mother. Or maybe me, for running out like that. 'What do you need to apologise for?'

'It was a bad idea taking you to see my parents.'

My brain freezes. A bad idea? To take me? My hands start to shake. I never thought Phil would be ashamed of me. He never seemed like he was before. But here he is, saying he shouldn't have taken me. He's still speaking but I can't take the words in. I'm a bad idea. It was me that was the problem. I didn't fit in. It feels like my life is crumbling apart. All the things I was relying on are shifting like sand.

'I've got to go,' I say, interrupting him. I hang up and sink onto a bench. Madge scampers round and round my feet, knotting the lead around my ankles. I let her. I'm in shock. I didn't think Phil would ever feel like that about me. Perhaps his mum told him things about me, and he believed her. Perhaps he now thinks I'm a bad influence on Maisie and Erin, and I shouldn't be allowed to see them anymore. Perhaps he's decided he doesn't want me as part of their family now since I obviously don't fit in.

It's my fault. I'm a bad idea.

CHAPTER 17
SASHA

Friday

Nell and I hit the shops hard! We both like shopping, but I'll admit, it's the fact every shop is air conditioned that really swings it for us. We thoroughly inspect every boutique, not wanting to rush back to the baked street outside.

'I wonder how the others are getting on,' says Nell as she looks along a rail of tops, flicking between them. 'I thought at least Cam might have caught up with us by now. You've not missed a call from her, have you?'

I check my phone. No missed calls. We walk out of the shop, the heat hitting us. It's the kind of heat that lets you know you're really on holiday.

'Let's find a drink,' says Nell.

We walk along a row of shops. There's a bridal one, the window brimming with ivory dresses, veils and mother-of-the-bride outfits. Dad's wedding is in two days. Two days. There's a heavy ball of worry in the centre of me. Am I doing the right thing?

Nell's slowed down and is pressing her face up against the glass. 'Oh, that one is lovely. My cousin got married last summer and she looked amazing. Hers was a bit like that one, only with less lace at the neck and a softer scoop in the neckline.'

I turn back, trying to sound interested and Definitely Not Stressed Out by even the mention of weddings. 'Oh, that's nice.' Dammit. I just sound bored.

'It was a lovely day. Jason, who she got married to, was dressed up really smart, like all the ushers and stuff. And they had a reception at this posh hotel. It was amazing. Weddings really are a totally happy event, aren't they?'

Unless of course your dad's awkward and stubborn like mine. And doesn't realise you're about to gate-crash his wedding.

I try and shake off the feeling. That feeling that I'm doing the wrong thing, that I'm going to make it all worse, that I'll ruin the day in a whole new and unexpected way.

'Sasha? Are you okay?' Nell's looking at me.

'Yeah, I'm fine.'

'Cos you seem a bit off.'

'Nah, I'm all good. Just tired from all the driving I guess.'

She looks at me and raises an eyebrow, knowing that's a half truth.

'I can't believe Dad's getting married. He's going to marry Clarisse. And I should be okay with that. And I sort of am. But it's going to change everything and it's really going to happen.'

'Just because he's getting married,' Nell says, 'doesn't mean he stops being your dad. He'll always be your dad. Nothing can change that.'

'But I've only just got back my relationship with him, after years and years,' I say.

Nell thinks for a moment. 'Was Clarisse with him, when he got back in touch?'

'Yes,' I say. 'They got together a few months before I saw them last summer.'

'Could it be,' says Nell, 'that Clarisse was the one who encouraged your dad to get back in touch?'

We turn the corner and come across a market,

the streets suddenly bustling with people, stalls lining the pavements, all piled high with produce of every sort.

'Wow!' says Nell. 'Look at the baker's stall. I've never seen loaves done like that before.' And she hurries off to examine them, leaving me to deal with what she's just said.

I follow her around the stalls as she exclaims over the range of cheeses, or the types of pies, or the assortment of cured meats. I can't seem to get excited about them somehow. The thought of turning up on Dad's wedding day is eating my brain. What if he doesn't want me there? What if he's secretly relieved I'm not going? After all, it wasn't him who called me. It was Clarisse.

Nell has finished looking and is stood in the shade of a bag stall. 'I'm boiled. Let's go and find a shady place to get that drink.'

'Good plan,' I say, getting out my phone. 'I'll call the others, see if they're ready to meet up.'

Cam answers quickly and says she'll come and find us. Hetal says she is about done and will be along in ten minutes.

We order a round of iced teas and sit at a little table in the shade of a huge Poplar tree. Cam arrives just after the drinks do. Madge is trotting along at her side.

'She is so adorable!' says Nell. 'She's really got the hang of it.'

Cam grins. 'Yeah. She loves it. And I do, too. I don't have to carry a small furry hot-water bottle anymore!'

We laugh and sip our drinks. Cam pours some water for Madge. She laps at it with her little pink tongue before exploring around our feet for a while. Having investigated as far as her lead will allow, she claws her way up Cam's leg and settles on her lap.

'Daft moggy,' she says, tickling her ears.

Hetal's coming along the street, beaming. Clearly she's had an amazing time at the church. She's out of breath by the time she gets to us.

'Good afternoon?' I ask.

'The best. Absolutely fascinating. But that's not my big news.'

'Tell us then,' says Nell, taking a sip of her drink.

'This really should start with a drum roll, but here goes. I've got us all tickets for a music festival, tomorrow in Montpellier! Isn't that wonderful?'

Cam sits up. 'Tickets to a festival? How much did those set you back?'

'Montpellier?' I ask. 'Is that on our way?'

Hetal laughs. 'It sort of is. Only downside is it will be quite a drive this afternoon.'

'How much of a drive?'

'Five hours?'

My heart sinks. We've already driven three hours this morning and I am *done* with driving.

'That's a long way for Sasha to drive,' says Nell. 'You should have checked first.'

'It was a brilliant offer though,' says Hetal. 'It'll be perfect. The bands that are playing are amazing. And they were his last four tickets. They would have gone if I hadn't bought them straightaway. And we can stop on the way.'

'Look, it doesn't matter, okay?' I say. 'It's done now.'

'How much were they?' asks Cam.

Hetal tells us and Cam whistles.

'But it's a really good deal, because it's so close to the festival. They should have been way more expensive,' insists Hetal.

Good deal or not, it's a massive chunk out of our trip's funds.

'You should have checked,' says Cam. 'That's a crazy amount of money.'

'Don't you want to go to a music festival?' snaps Hetal, her face flushed.

'Yeah, sure. But for me, that's not the only question I have to ask myself. Otherwise I'd be doing all sorts of things. But like most other people, I also have to ask questions like, *can I afford this? Is this a priority for me? Wouldn't I prefer to eat?*'

There's a deathly silence.

'If you feel like that,' says Hetal, 'I'll pay for the tickets.'

'Don't be stupid,' says Cam. 'I'm not wanting charity. I'll pay for my ticket. I just would have liked a say, that's all.'

'On the upside,' I say, trying to lighten the mood, 'we do now get to enjoy an amazing music festival.'

'I'm probably going to sit it out,' says Nell. 'You know. Crowds. They're not my thing.'

We all know crowds aren't her thing. Including Hetal.

Cam's rolling her eyes. Hetal looks on the verge of tears. But it's her own fault. She should have checked.

CHAPTER 18
HETAL

Friday

No one says anything on the way back to the car. It's even worse once we've set off. Cam just sticks her AirPods in and looks out of the window. I was trying to do something nice. How was I to know they were all going to react like that? I'm trying so hard to make this the perfect road trip, but it seems like the more I try, the worse it gets.

'Which way, Hetal?' says Sasha suddenly. We're at a junction and I have no idea which way.

'Sorry! Let me check.' I frantically click open Google Maps. The car behind honks its horn.

'Don't worry, I've got it,' says Cam who's gesticulating wildly through the back window. Nell laughs awkwardly.

I can't laugh. It's like the joy has been squashed by the weight of timetables, maps and plans and has got stuck underneath it all. And I still have to make sure we have a campsite for tonight in Montpellier, which given there's a festival on, might be tricky. I daren't mention it though. Everyone's likely to have another go at me.

The car toots again and overtakes, the driver shaking his fist at us.

'Ignore him,' Nell says to Sasha.

'Ignore who?' she says, grinning.

At last I figure out which way. 'Turn right, then immediate left,' I say.

Sasha follows my instructions and in a few seconds we're back cruising along the road south. I start searching for campsites in Montpellier. I've not done nearly enough research and I'm terrified. I find one. The website looks good but there are zero reviews. What if it's like the cow campsite? Or worse?

I flick back to the website I was reading. Places to eat. I skim through it, trying to find the best place to go this evening. We deserve an evening out, after everything. And we're less likely to get food poisoning if the food is professionally cooked. I cringe just thinking about how ill I made everyone. I cringe when I think about the last campsite. And I cringe when I think about our failed trip to the church.

The Collegiate Church of Saint Martin is fifth century. How can you not be excited by something that's existed that long? I don't know what else I can do except try harder. But at least we've now got the music festival – and despite everything they've said, I bet they'll love it. It's going to be the thing that brings us all together.

'I love this song,' says Cam, and turns the music up. She sings along loudly, with Nell joining in.

'All the practice at the deli has certainly improved my singing,' she says after reaching a note none of us can manage.

They all laugh, though it doesn't sound natural. Are we all just going to forget the worst argument we've had? The only argument? I try hard to concentrate on the website.

'Not feeling like singing?' asks Sasha, eyeing me sideways as she drives.

'Not at the moment, just trying to read,' I say.

'You've got to lighten up,' says Cam from the back.

Her words stick in me like a knife. That's me

entirely. I can't lighten up. I'm a killjoy. I take all the joy out of the situation. I'm too busy fussing and flapping about details and lists and folders. Nobody wants that person at a party. Nobody wants that person on a holiday.

Focusing on the words is much harder when they're blurred by tears. No one notices. They're all too busy singing and laughing and arguing over what the words are. I start to Google what the lyrics are but stop myself. Nobody likes a know-it-all.

After driving for hours, we finally pull into the campsite and slowly drive down the field to our pitch. I found one with availability, but did that mean it was going to be awful? I quickly check it over and breathe out. It's fine. No broken glass, no rubbish, no cows on the loose.

'This looks the business!' says Cam, looking all around her. She's right. I hadn't noticed as I was so fixated on the pitch. The area is beautiful, with trees along one side and rolling countryside as far as you can see, with a line of sea drawn along the horizon.

'We're going to have to peg the tent down well,' I say. 'I bet the wind whips across there from the sea.'

'Ai, ai, captain,' says Sasha.

Is she mocking me? I open the boot and start to get everything out. The sooner we set up, the sooner we can relax into our evening, but Cam and Nell are already stretched out on the grass, Madge gambolling around them.

'Let's put up the tent,' I say.

'Yeah, in a minute,' says Cam, sleepily. 'There's no rush.'

Nell's not moving either, and Sasha's walked off to explore the rest of the campsite. Well, I can at least make a start. How hard can it be?

I empty the boot and unearth the tent. I've already put it up once so it shouldn't be so hard to do it again. I shake open the tent, gather the pegs into a pile and read the instructions. I thread poles and tug on lines and nearly ... have ... it ... when it collapses completely.

'Stupid thing,' I mutter, the sweat dripping down my back. I wish I was lying on the cool grass in the shade while someone else sorts out the tent. Then it twigs. Why shouldn't I? I leave the tent in a mangled heap and throw myself on the ground next to Cam.

'We'll do it in a minute,' mutters Cam, without me even saying anything.

'Fine. Whenever,' I say. I am now going to be super-chilled Hetal. Nothing-stresses-her-out Hetal. Totally horizontal Hetal.

I last about ten minutes before sitting up.

'Come on,' I say. 'It'll only take us a few minutes.'

'Stop stressing. If it'll only take us a few minutes, why do we have to do it now?' says Cam.

I sigh and roll onto my stomach and scroll on my phone. I've tried. There's nothing more I can do.

It gets dark without us really noticing. Dusk kind of creeps up on you. You think it's still light until, bang, you can't see a thing.

Sasha comes back. 'Haven't you put the tent up?'

Cam sits up. 'Daaaammmmnnn, it's dark.'

I bite my tongue So Hard.

We all get up and start pulling the tent into position. It's ten times harder in the dark. You can't see which bit is which and it takes us several minutes to realise it's actually upside down.

'We should have done this earlier,' I mutter.

'Yeah, well, we didn't,' says Cam. 'Get over it.'

Once the tent's up, I check the opening times of the café I found. It shut half an hour ago.

'What are we doing for food, Hetal?' asks Cam.

'I'm just finding somewhere,' I reply, searching for somewhere that'll still be open. I find a place, but it doesn't look amazing.

'Not like you not to have a plan,' says Sasha.

'I had a plan, but it's all been set back because we were late putting up the tent.'

'Chillax,' says Cam. 'We're on holiday.'

'I am quite hungry, though,' says Nell. 'Have you found somewhere near that does food, Hetal?'

'Yep,' I say. I take a deep breath, trying to be cool and chilled and relaxed. 'It's open for another half hour, so let's go.'

We zip up the tent, shove our things into the car and set off across the campsite. The sky is clear above us, and you can see the stars coming out. The moon's nearly full and you can even see Jupiter if you look closely. It's weird to think that looking up into the night sky is looking into infinity. There's no end to what's above us. And that kind of puts it all into perspective. Cam's right. It doesn't matter that we put the tent up in the dark. It doesn't matter which café we go to. It doesn't matter if we don't quite follow the plan. We're on holiday, together, and that's what matters.

We reach the café, and I frown. It's all in darkness and the car park's empty.

Cam turns to me. 'What now, Hetal?'

I fight with all my being to hold the scream of frustration inside me, all the star-zen vanishing in an instant.

CHAPTER 19
NELL

Friday

I've got to speak to Tom. I take my chance when everyone's in the supermarket getting food. I borrow Sasha's phone and video call him. It's ringing. I lean against the recycling bins and hope and hope that he answers.

'Hello?'

'Hi. It's me.'

'Who?'

I feel my face flame. 'It's me. Nell.'

'Nell! Sorry, didn't recognise your voice. And it's really dark. I can barely see you.'

Or he's forgotten me.

Thanks, brain. Helpful.

'So, how's things?' I now realise I have no idea what I want to say. I can't just launch into asking about Ariel and what's going on with her. 'How's work?'

'You seriously didn't just call me, from France, to ask me how work's going.' He laughs. He's at the beach, I can just make out the sea glinting in the moonlight behind him. Then I catch something. There's a second person laughing in the background. Who is it? I can't ask; I'd look completely paranoid.

'How's the trip? How's France?'

I smile. 'It's hot. And brilliant. The campsite we're staying at tonight is lovely.'

'Funny. It looks like you're hanging out by the bins.'

I'm glad he can't see me too well, as my face is on fire.

'Just waiting while the others buy food.' He's talking quietly to someone off camera. And I'm just waiting for him to finish, like an idiot.

I can't do this.

The others are still inside, so I lie. 'Anyway, here they come now. See you when I get back.' I hang up.

Who was he with? Why didn't he say he wasn't on his own? And why couldn't I think of anything to say? That's not great. What if it was Ariel? They'll be having a good laugh at stupid Nell who rings with nothing to say, who's hanging out by the bins.

A text pops up.

Sorry that was short. I do miss you. You just caught me while I was out with a friend. Hope to catch up with you soon. x

A friend? Why not say who? But I guess he wouldn't if it was Ariel. Is this jealousy? It's awful, like your thoughts are eating your brain, like everything feels wrong and against you. I've got to stop.

No problem. Enjoy your evening.

Unless of course you're with Ariel, in which case I hope you have an awful time and it's all her fault and you remember why you finished with her.

The others come out of the shop, carrying bags of food, and laughing. Have they managed to sort out some of the stuff going on? Hetal's been really quiet all afternoon. I go and join them and together we walk back to the campsite. We unzip the tent, but sit outside, the heat unbearable inside.

There hasn't been another message from Tom. He clearly took my message seriously and is busy enjoying his evening.

'Thanks for your phone, Sasha,' I say, handing it back.

'Everything okay with Tom?' she asks.

I nod. No point in bothering Sasha with it. She'd tell me to cut my losses and get out of it with limited pain.

Sasha opens the bags and pulls out crusty bread, butter twisted in paper, a jar of raspberry conserve and some slices of salami. We crunch and tear our way through.

Hetal's still really quiet so maybe we haven't moved on.

'I think I'm going to bed,' she says.

'Everything okay?' asks Sasha.

'Yeah. Just tired. Night everyone.'

She goes into the tent, and I hear her shuffling around, getting ready for bed.

'Think I'm going to call it a night too,' says Sasha and follows Hetal in.

'You tired as well?' asks Cam.

'Me? Not especially.' My brain's wired, thinking about Tom and his 'friend'.

Madge is curled up in Cam's lap, having eaten the cat food Cam fed her. She really is a cute kitten.

Cam's still not said what happened with her grandparents. Perhaps she doesn't know how.

'Any time you want to talk,' I say, 'I'm here.'

Cam looks across at me, eyebrows raised.

'Only you haven't said how it went with your grandparents.'

'Nothing to talk about,' she says. 'You know what, I am tired after all.' And without another word, she gets up and disappears into the tent.

Perhaps I should have left it, but there's clearly something bugging her. I know Cam can sometimes be a private person, but it's only me. The person who went with her to find her birth father. The person who knows what that means to her. What happened with her grandparents that was so awful she had to leave? And why isn't she talking about it? I've seen her in the car, cancelling phone calls. Who's ringing and why isn't she speaking to them?

I lean back and look up at the sky. The four of us don't seem to be getting closer, in fact, I don't think we've been further apart. And it's not just drifting apart – our friendship took a battering today. That isn't what's supposed to happen on a road trip. We're supposed to be having the most amazing time ever and our friendships should be the strongest they've ever been. But we're falling apart.

And then there's Tom. There's definitely something going on there. And if it is Ariel, there's nothing I can do about it all the way from France.

There's no way I could stand losing my friends *and* Tom in one holiday.

I get up and start to put the food away and gather up our stuff for the night. Sasha's left her phone on top of the rug she was sitting on. I check for messages. She wouldn't mind. She's said over and over until my phone's fixed, I can use hers. But there's nothing.

I flick open Instagram and check Ariel's page. It's a selfie. Her hair looks amazing and her face is alive against the backdrop of a moonlit beach.

I've had the best evening rekindling an old friendship.

I can't fool myself any longer. It feels like the world has crashed down on my head. Tom and Ariel are back together. I try to cry quietly so I don't disturb the others.

CHAPTER 20
CAM

Saturday

I'm the first awake and I can hear the others are still asleep. There's the regular rise and fall of breathing from all of them. I don't want to disturb them but equally I need to get out of here. The stifling heat of the tent and the gentle crushing of being too close to other people all the time is the thing that gets me out of my sleeping bag.

These friends are everything I have left, so why I am feeling like this? I think about yesterday. Why didn't I tell Nell when she asked about my grandparents? We used to be so close, I'd tell her anything. Am I protecting our friendship by not telling her? Besides, this trip isn't about me. We're here to have an amazing road trip, and to get Sasha to a wedding. No one wants me whinging about my problems. I pull on some clothes and quietly unzip the tent.

No one stirs.

Madge and I make our way across the campsite as everyone is starting to wake up. There's a smell of coffee and frying bacon and I'm suddenly starving. I walk down to the shops we found last night and there's a café open. I go in and pick something off the menu and order it in dodgy French. I know it's dodgy because the girl behind the counter is hiding her laughter. I probably asked for something outrageous by accident.

I find a seat outside and sit down with my steaming cup of coffee and my warm croissant. This is better. Time to think. Time to breathe. Time to just be me. No one telling me what I should be doing, or saying, or thinking. Madge doesn't count. She literally doesn't care who I am, or whether I'm their granddaughter or not, or whether I should have pink hair or not.

Pink hair.

I smile as I think about Leo, the cute boy from the pet shop. I've still got his number, carefully tucked into my wallet. We're now miles away from his town, but if we'd stayed, would I have called him?

Just the thought of calling him makes my heart beat faster. Why shouldn't I call him anyway? So far this holiday, my family stuff has bombed, my friendships seriously aren't delivering – something's got to go right.

Before I have a chance to second guess myself, I find the receipt, get out my phone and dial the number. After all, he did say to call him.

It rings three times then someone answers.

'*Allo, oui?*'

Ah crap. I'd forgotten he'd be speaking French.

'*Ah bonjour,*' I say in my Very Best French.

There's a beat, then he laughs.

'Hello! You rang.'

I can hear the smile in his voice.

'How do you know who it is?' I'm smiling too.

'Lucky guess. Plus, your French accent is … one on its own.'

'Rude.' But probably true tbh.

'How is your kitten doing? Madge wasn't it?'

He remembered.

'She's brilliant. And she loves her lead. It's been a literal lifesaver.'

'So you have not rung to complain about the lead?'

'No,' I say. Why had I rung? Because the rest of my life is currently a car wreck and I kind of need some strings-free, feel-good cuteness in my life. Probably too honest.

'Do you have other pet supplies that you require?'

'No.' I'm smiling again.

'May I ask then, why are you calling me?'

'You gave me your number and it seemed a waste not to ring it.'

Leo laughs.

'Are you still in town?'

'No, sadly not. We're in Montpellier. My friend got tickets for the music festival today.'

'Ah she was lucky to get them – that festival is amazing.'

I thought for a minute. Nell said yesterday that she probably wouldn't be going to the festival. She doesn't like crowds. So that means we technically have a spare ticket.

'I don't suppose you can get here? We have a spare ticket.'

Leo's quiet for a moment, probably working out whether that's even possible. It's a really long way to travel on a whim.

'Okay,' he says finally.

'Okay, you can come? Or okay, crazy lady, hang up now?'

'Okay, I can come. I'll swap my shift and drive down. Which campsite are you at?'

I tell him and we arrange to meet later and I hang up, my hands sweaty and my heart pounding. How can just talking to someone on the phone do that to a person? I can't believe he's coming. Here. Today.

CHAPTER 21
SASHA

Saturday

Hetal's talking nearly non-stop about the music festival, and I feel like I can't breathe. Dad's wedding is tomorrow. Tomorrow. It's like this big lump of pressure is sat on me and I can't move, or think, or do anything. I've got this far. I might ruin his wedding. I might mess up the day. But I've got to be there. Not late, not half-hearted. I will be mature about it and I will do my very best not to ruin it.

I ought to tell everyone how I feel. They'd know what to say, know what I should do. So why can't I? All I have to do is open my mouth and say the words, 'I'm freaking out about Dad's wedding tomorrow' and everyone would understand.

Hetal's still talking about the music festival.

'And then on the second stage, there's the indie bands playing, and I thought we could go to that one after lunch. There are some really amazing acts performing.' Hetal shows Cam the list and she leans in.

'That is actually really cool.'

Hetal beams. Guess she's relieved that Cam's not mad with her anymore.

We're all getting ready to go out to the festival. We've had the debate over shoes (comfort or style) and outfit (strappy and burn vs covered and overheat); Cam's taking Madge, and has to take a bag big enough to fit enough water and snacks for her.

'Which bands are you looking forward to, Sasha?' says Nell.

'Erm, all of them?' I say. I'm not sure I'm that convincing.

'Is there something wrong?' asks Hetal. She's frowning like when she can't solve a puzzle.

'No, everything's fine.'

'Yeah, and I'm the Pope,' says Cam. 'I know you think you're good at hiding your emotions, but actually you suck at it. Something's eating at you. So, what's up?'

She seems in a better mood since she came back from her walk this morning. Guess the heat and the travelling got to us all yesterday. 'I'm just a bit stressed about tomorrow. I don't want to mess things up for Dad. I've been starting to think it would be better I didn't go.'

'Nonsense,' says Hetal, matter-of-factly. 'Your dad will be really pleased to have you there. You're his daughter. Of course you must go.'

'Not to mention, we've all trailed our arses across France for this wedding. There's no way you're ducking out of it now,' says Cam.

'Well, I have to go,' says Nell. 'I have a phone to collect.'

We all laugh.

'Which bits are you worried about?' says Nell. 'I find it helpful to be specific, then I can sort out each part of my worry, one at a time.'

'I'm worried I'll be late, mainly. We're miles away from Marseilles. What if there's a hold-up on the way, or we get lost.'

Hetal gets out her phone and taps on it. 'Journey time is two hours seventeen minutes. Let's allow three and a half hours. I know it's a Sunday morning, but we want to play it safe. When and where is the wedding?'

'At noon at *La Maison de la Falaise*.'

Hetal thinks for a moment. 'You'll want to get there in plenty of time. To be on the safe side, we need to be away from the campsite at eight.'

'Eight?' Cam sounds horrified. 'With the tent down and everything packed? On the morning after a music festival?'

Hetal nods.

'I'm sorry, everyone—,' I start, but Nell interrupts me.

'No need to apologise. We're in this amazing place *because* we're here to support you. You need to be at your dad's wedding. And that is what you're going to do. We can manage eight.'

Hetal nods, but Cam doesn't look so sure.

'So, that's the timings all sorted. What else?' Nell asks.

Dare I share my deepest fear?

'What if...' I start. This is hard. 'What if Dad doesn't actually want me there? What if rather than proving I'm reliable and mature, I actually end up ruining the day instead? I'll mess up the seating plan, the photos, all their plans...'

'I'm sure that won't be true,' says Hetal, though she doesn't sound convinced. She knows it would mess up carefully made plans.

'Sorry, don't ask me about fathers,' says Cam. 'Total mystery to me.'

Nell frowns and looks at Cam. I wonder again what's going on with her.

'Does your dad love you?' asks Nell.

'Yes, I guess, in his own way,' I answer.

'Well, that's all that matters,' says Nell.

I desperately hope she's right.

'Nell,' says Cam. 'Yesterday you said you were thinking of not going to the festival. Is that still the plan?'

Nell nods. 'I'll walk into town with you but the whole queueing, turnstiles, crushing crowds thing isn't my scene. I'll come back to the tent and just chill for the day. I'll be fine,' she adds as she sees my expression. 'Really.'

'I thought that's what you'd say,' says Cam. 'Because I've kind of invited someone along to have your ticket.'

What? Who the heck does she know in France?

Hetal is the first in with the question. 'Who have you invited?'

'The cute guy from the pet shop.'

We all just stare at her.

'From the pet shop yesterday?' says Hetal slowly. 'Someone you've only met once?'

Cam's nodding as if this is the most normal thing in the world.

Hetal's mad. You can see it in every part of her face.

'You assumed that Nell wouldn't want her ticket. You assumed that we,' she gestured to me, 'would be fine spending the day with some rando you'd found—'

'Just chill, Hetal,' Cam says. 'It'll be fine.'

Hetal almost spits Cam's words from yesterday back at her. 'You should have checked first.'

CHAPTER 22
HETAL

Saturday

I can't believe Cam. This holiday is supposed to be just for us. How could she invite some random guy she met to come and spend the day with us? And if she tells me to chill one more time, I swear I'm going to lose it.

The guy's called Leo, and evidently we're meeting him in town now, so we set off. It's not far into Montpellier from where we've camped and there will probably be lots of pre-music festival stuff going on. I suppose it'll be good to get the vibe early in the day. It's different from everywhere we've been so far; it feels more sophisticated. I suppose it is the South of France, renowned for its celeb-appeal.

'I wonder if we'll see anyone famous,' says Nell, her eyes wide.

'What? Just out and about?' says Cam. 'That would be cool.'

'Let's keep a lookout,' says Nell. 'What do you reckon, Sasha? You ever seen anyone famous here?'

'No,' says Sasha. 'Though I haven't been to Montpellier before.'

I spot a marquee in the town square. It's an information point for the music festival. 'Let's go over and see if we can find out some more about it.'

'Seriously?' says Cam. 'We already know *so much*. Why would we need to know more?' But she follows us anyway.

Sasha's volunteered to translate for me. She's busy chatting away to the woman. I'm picking up the odd word, but not really sure what she's saying.

Sasha turns to me. 'That's odd. She's just said the tickets sold out months ago. She's really surprised we managed to get any.'

I frown. The stall I'd bought them from had looked legit. 'Is she sure?' I swing my bag off my shoulder and dig out the tickets.

Sasha takes them off me and hands them to the woman, who examines them. Then she shakes her head and says something to Sasha.

'What's she saying?' I ask but have a creeping realisation that I already know.

The tickets are fakes.

And not even very good ones at that.

The woman's very sympathetic but there's nothing she can do.

How could I have been so stupid? I'd usually check and double-check this sort of thing, but it must have been the excitement, or the desperation to find something amazing to do. I can't believe I just threw our money away.

The woman hands the tickets back to me and pats me on the arm.

'She says not to beat yourself up. You're not the first person to fall for the scam.'

I thank her and walk away, aware that the others are speaking.

'Sasha, did she tell you how to get the money back?' It's Cam.

'We can't,' says Sasha.

'What? So we've lost all that money, and can't even get into the festival?'

I rip up the tickets and dump them into a bin on my way past. Why am I even here? I'm not any fun, but if I'm not even any good at organising stuff, then what is the point? This was supposed to be the highlight, the feel-good moment we're all desperate for, and now what? I can hear Cam in my head, mocking my original plan for the historical tour of the city.

I find a shady bench and drop onto it. Sasha sits down beside me, followed by the others.

'Oh no,' Cam groans. 'What am I going to tell Leo? He's travelling all this way to go to the festival.'

I can't listen to her. I just can't.

'I'm going to go back to the tent,' I say. 'You guys stay here. Shop, eat, whatever. I've just remembered I didn't put sun cream on.'

No one stops me from leaving. I take Madge with me and trudge back to the campsite, the sun high in the sky, everything bleached in the sunshine. I've got to face it. I'm hopeless. I can't organise things. I can't spot a scammer. I can't do the right things for my friends, my family or even my boyfriend. I let everyone down.

I sit, leaning against a tree on the campsite with Madge curled up beside me and watch people coming and going. No one else seems to be stressing about plans. No one else is carrying a binder full of notes. No one else is looking at the time and hurrying up.

I feel so tired of everything. So tired of running to not get anywhere.

CHAPTER 23
NELL

Saturday

It's less awkward now Hetal's gone back to the campsite. You could almost see the stress coming off her. Cam suggests we have ice creams as she's literally dying of heat exhaustion. I'm not sure ice cream is a recognised treatment for heat exhaustion, but me and Sasha go along with it. It's too hot to argue.

We eat them in a shady spot, though they're still melting faster than we can eat them.

'I can't believe Hetal,' says Cam, pushing her hair back from her face and lifting it up around her neck. 'What a waste of time and money.'

'And loads of extra travelling which we didn't need to do,' says Sasha. 'We could have been in

Marseille by now, chilling out, just down the road from the wedding venue.'

'I'm worried about Hetal. It's not like her to be upset,' I say.

'She wasn't upset. She went back because she'd forgotten to put sun cream on,' says Cam.

'Really?' I say. 'Don't forget this is Hetal we're talking about. *She* reminded *me* to put it on this morning.'

'In which case, she wants to be on her own,' says Cam. 'If she wanted us with her, she'd have said, right?'

I frown. I think it's different with Hetal. I don't think she'd say. But I don't tell Cam that.

'So, are we staying in town then?' asks Sasha.

She always looks impossibly cool, even in this insane heat. I just feel like a hot mess. Even Cam's looking good, her pink hair arranged with the perfect amount of casual style.

'Leo should be here any minute,' says Cam, looking at her phone. 'I'm cringing at the thought of telling him the festival is off.'

I exchange a glance with Sasha. What are we supposed to do? Hang out with Cam and her pet-shop boy, checking he's not some kind of nutcase, or can we just go off and do our own thing?

Cam's now scanning the people walking past us, until she shouts something and jumps up. I've never known her like this. She walks over to someone who seems to recognise her. Cam wasn't wrong. He is cute. He leans into Cam and kisses her on both cheeks.

'Leo, I presume,' says Sasha, shading her eyes so she can get a proper look.

'Well, I would hope so, otherwise, this has taken a turn for the even weirder,' I say and Sasha laughs.

'Are we supposed to babysit them?' I ask.

'No, surely not. I don't get why she invited him. This is our road trip – how did she not know it was weird? Let's check him out first, see if his vibes are off, then split. There's no way I'm spending the day with them.'

'Okay, good plan,' I say as Cam and Leo head over to our bench.

'Good afternoon,' says Leo, smiling at both me and Sasha. 'Nice to meet you.'

He turns to Cam. 'Was there another friend? You said there were four of you?'

'Oh, Hetal,' says Cam. 'No, she's gone back to the campsite.'

'So, Leo,' says Sasha. 'You like our friend, Cam?'

Leo frowns a little. 'I like Cam? Yes.'

'Why?' asks Sasha.

'What the hell, Sasha?' says Cam. She's still smiling but giving Sasha daggers.

Leo seems to be weighing up Sasha. I think he gets it.

'She has pink hair and loves her cat. And I want to know what else is amazing about her. Is that a crime?'

Cam is speechless. Sasha grins.

'Smile,' says Sasha, holding up her phone. And she takes a photo of Leo next to Cam. 'Okay, so if you hurt our friend In. Any. Way. We'll hand this photo over to the police *and* we will personally hunt you down. Got it?'

'Got it,' says Leo.

'And I'm really sorry – we got scammed. We can't go to the festival. We've only just found out. I'm sorry you've travelled all this way for nothing,' says Cam.

'I tell you a secret. It wasn't really the festival I was here for.' Leo's looking at Cam like me and Sasha aren't here.

'Now why don't you kids run along and have fun,' says Sasha in her best American-sitcom voice.

Leo laughs.

'I can't believe you!' says Cam, play punching Sasha on her arm.

'I can't believe you did that either,' I say. That could have seriously backfired.

'Well,' says Sasha, shrugging, 'Nell and I decided we didn't want to tag along on your "date" or whatever this is. So, you're welcome. Go and have an amazing time.'

'Okay. Thanks guys. This has been … embarrassing. See you later.' And they disappear into the crowd together.

'And then there were two,' says Sasha. 'I can't believe we've lost all that money. We could have had a serious shopping spree with that cash. Now we're going to have to really cut back on what else we can do on this road trip.'

'Yeah, and if we'd gone straight to Marseille, I could have picked up my new phone a day early. If only she'd have thought before she decided to buy those tickets.'

'You fancy a cold water?' asks Sasha.

'Always, this heat is dehydrating me faster than I can drink.'

'Coming right up then.'

'Could I borrow your phone again?' I ask. I hate having to always ask. At least there's only one more day until I get my new one.

'No problem.' She passes it to me. 'Though there

haven't been any messages.' She walks towards a stall selling drinks from an enormous trough of ice.

I check for messages anyway, just to make sure. Tom knows it's Sasha's phone so probably doesn't want to send one. Probably.

I check out Ariel's page. I don't know why I do it to myself, but I have to know, like picking a scab. I can't leave it alone.

My heart stops.

There's no doubt this time.

It's there.

The proof of what I suspected. A photo of her and Tom, arms round each other, his lips pressed to her cheek, Ariel grinning into the camera. Like she's mocking me. It feels like the world has stopped. Everyone and everything has stopped where they are. It's true. It's real. It's proof.

The caption underneath simply says:

True love

What do I do? What *can* I do? How could he? But what if Ariel and Tom are meant to be together? They've a much longer history. What if I'm just the blip in *their* relationship, that thing that comes along to make them realise they're supposed to be together? My heart is thundering in my chest and my head is pounding. I don't want this to be true. I feel like everything's crashing around me. I'm such an idiot for believing he could like me, would want to be with me. I bet they're laughing at me. Naïve, unsuspecting, trusting Nell. Not got a clue.

My hands shake as I type.

I can't believe what you've done. It's over. We're over. I'm done.

I flick the phone off and hand it back to Sasha who has returned holding two bottles of water. 'Thanks.' I want to say I won't be borrowing it again, but I'm not sure I can stand the relationship post-mortem.

My hand is shaking as I open the bottle. Sasha's saying something about tomorrow but her voice is a blur.

'Sasha, if you don't mind, I think I need to clear my head a bit. I'll see you back at the campsite later, okay?'

Sasha looks surprised. 'Oh, alright then. Everything okay?'

'Yeah, everything's great.'

I walk off down the street. There are loads of people, but it feels like I'm not really here. Just floating between them. Like I'm in a parallel world, where everyone in that world is happy and having a great day. And I'm stuck in this one, where there's no escape from how I'm feeling.

I walk and walk and walk. Turning down streets and following the crowds, until I realise.

I have no idea where I am.

CHAPTER 24
CAM

Saturday

We talk – Leo and I – a surprising amount, especially considering the language gap. Thank goodness for the translation app on my phone. It takes a bit of getting used to but it's worth it. Turns out we have a ton of stuff in common. We start off basic – music, food, what we like doing. Then move onto the big stuff. The stuff that really matters. Plans for the future, where we want to travel, how we feel about our families. That it's got a bit weird with my mates. All that.

Perhaps it's easier to share when there's a good chance you're never going to see this person again. There's no vested interest. He doesn't know me or anyone I'm talking about. But he listens. He listens like my words are oxygen and he can't get enough.

He's told me about his sister who is sick. And how much he loves her and wishes she could get better. But also how he feels guilty that he likes going to work so he doesn't have to think about her being sick for a bit. I get it. It's an escape.

Sometime in the afternoon he grabs my hand to get my attention. There are street performers and one is about to eat fire. We watch and he doesn't let go.

We've walked and walked. Leo has been to Montpellier a couple of times before but not since he was younger, so neither of us really have a clue about where we are or what there is to do in the town. But that doesn't seem to matter.

'Do you want to find somewhere to eat?' asks Leo.

I look at my phone and realise the hours have flown by. And that I am actually pretty hungry.

We stop and get tacos, sitting on a low wall, watching the world go by.

'I'm so pleased you called me,' he says when we're finished eating. 'I don't usually give out my number. But there was something about you.'

'I don't usually call numbers when I'm given them,' I say.

We sit, just looking at each other. It feels weird to have this connection with someone, discovered so randomly, in the middle of another country.

A big drop of rain falls on the ground in front of us. Then another and another. It's about to chuck it down and we're going to get soaked if we don't move fast.

We run together, across the square to the covered doorway of a small church. The sky is split in two by a brilliant flash of lightning and almost immediately we're deafened by an enormous clap of thunder. We skid into the porch, laughing and out of breath. My hair is dripping wet and I'm soaked. I can't believe how fast this storm has come on.

It's mid-afternoon, but the grey storm clouds have made it dark. The lightning flashes again and again, the thunder loud enough to vibrate the world.

Leo stands beside me, watching the storm too. His eyes widen with every flash, every clap. That's another thing we have in common: a love of storms.

I reach for his hand, and he holds mine in his.

It's not until I pull his hand closer that his attention moves from the storm to me. I take a step towards him. A small, half step. A lift on my toes. A stretch up.

The last thing I see is his eyes widen as he realises what's happening is about to be way more interesting than the storm.

At first, it's me kissing him. Then he joins in, leaning into me, tangling his fingers into my hair and getting lost with me in the moment.

I can't believe this is happening.

We break off, and I smile at him.

'Seemed like the right thing to do,' I say.

'Felt like the right thing to me too,' says Leo, smiling and kissing me again.

We lose some more minutes.

The storm's still overhead, and the rain is now hammering down on the hot pavement all around us. Leo stops kissing me.

'Is that your phone?'

It is. I've been ignoring it.

I take it out of my back pocket. It's Hetal. It's probably nothing. Freaking out over some detail or other. I dismiss the call and smile at Leo.

I'm about to put my phone away when it rings again. This time it's Sasha. I frown. Why are they both trying to call me?

'Hello?'

'Oh, thank goodness you answered,' says Sasha. She sounds panicked.

'Yeah, sure,' I say. 'What's up?'

'Is Nell with you?'

'Nell? No, why?'

'Only we've not seen her for hours. Not since you left with Leo.'

'I thought she was with you?'

'No, she went off by herself.'

I check the time. It's been four hours. And now there's a massive storm and Nell's somewhere out in it.

'I'm sure she's fine,' I say, but I'm not convincing. She hasn't got a phone, so if she needs help, she can't even call us. And it's not even like she's had loads of experience about being away from home, with her mum being so over-protective. Crap. Her mum's going to kill us. 'Look, we'll come back to the campsite. Then we can figure out what to do.'

'Everything alright?' asks Leo as I hang up.

'Not really. Nell's missing.'

CHAPTER 25
SASHA

Saturday

I wipe the rain off my forehead and out of my eyes and search the field, looking for any sign of Nell. There's not a soul anywhere; everyone's sensibly sheltering in their tents.

'Come back in,' shouts Hetal over the roar of thunder and the rain pelting down.

I push back through the flap of the tent and zip it shut behind me. The noise of the rain on the canvas roof is deafening.

'No sign of her?' asks Hetal. I don't know why she's even asking.

I've no idea where Nell could be. She left me in town and told me she'd see me later at the campsite.

I should have lent her my phone. I should have checked she knew her way back. I should have agreed a time at least.

'She probably lost track of the time,' I say to Hetal, 'and now she's sheltering until the storm's passed.'

Hetal nods.

Thing is, if I'm thinking the worst, Hetal definitely will be.

Hetal's asked me a dozen times where was the last place I saw her, and when, and how she was feeling. I've been asked so many times I'm beginning to doubt myself. Did I miss something? Did she see something while she had my phone?

Hetal's quiet, searching things on her phone. The inside of the tent lights up with the lightning, then almost immediately thunder crashes again. It must be right above us.

'Tents are safe in a storm, aren't they?' I ask, as a particularly loud crack of thunder coincides exactly with a bright flash of lightning.

'Very safe. And we don't have metal poles, which is a plus. If anything, it's more likely to hit the tree we were under earlier.'

That makes me feel better. Until I think about Nell again and realise she's out in this.

'We need a plan,' Hetal says. 'We can't just sit here.'

'Cam said they were coming back straight away. Let's decide on what to do ready for when they're here. Then at least everyone knows what's happening and we won't lose anyone else.'

Hetal nods and is tapping away on her phone again.

There's a scrabbling at the tent zip.

I rush to open it. Maybe it's Nell back … but no, it's just Cam and Leo who cram into the tent, soaked to the skin and dripping all over everything.

I see Hetal shudder as our beds start to get wet.

'You're here. Thank goodness,' I say.

'We came as soon as you rang,' says Cam.

'As soon as you answered,' mutters Hetal under her breath.

Cam hears and looks like she's going to say something.

'We need to go and look for Nell,' I say. 'That's what's important now. Nothing else.'

Both Cam and Hetal decide to leave it.

'I think someone ought to stay here, in case Nell finds her way back. Are we working on the assumption that she's lost?' asks Cam.

That's the question Hetal and I had been

avoiding since we noticed that Nell had been gone a long time.

'I think so, yes,' I say. The alternatives are all too awful to even think about.

'I have my car,' says Leo. 'I can drive and Cam can look out for Nell. We can check a big area.'

'Good idea,' says Cam.

'I don't think someone needs to stay here,' says Hetal. 'Let's leave a big note saying we're all out looking for her, so to stay here until we get back. And we can check back every now and again to see if she's turned up.'

'Good idea,' I say. 'We could use my car.'

'Or we could check on the paths around the campsite,' says Hetal. 'She might be closer than we think.'

Cam and Leo disappear into the rain, promising to stay in touch, and Hetal scribbles a note, much of which is in capitals. Which is fair.

Then we're out into the overcast afternoon. The rain has eased a bit; it no longer stings as it hits your skin. We walk across the field together, Hetal looking all around her, backwards and forwards, trying to see if Nell could be there. She could be disorientated somewhere on the campsite. She may have made it back and then couldn't figure out which way it was. She may have stopped to shelter from the rain. We search as we walk, scanning the hedgerows and field for any signs of Nell.

'Nell!' calls Hetal. 'NELL!'

No one answers. Nell doesn't appear from under a tree or behind a hedge.

'Nell!' both me and Hetal call. We walk and shout as we go down the road.

Only the thunder replies, rumbling in the distance.

Hetal is ahead of me, frantically looking from side to side, looking into all the places Nell could be, and some places she couldn't possibly be. She turns back to me, her face screwed up.

'This is all my fault.'

I walk up to her and hug her tight. 'Of course this isn't your fault. It's nobody's fault. There are a thousand reasonable explanations why Nell hasn't come back yet. And none of them are your fault.'

Hetal's sobbing uncontrollably, her whole body shaking. She's clearly way more on edge than I realised. I think of the times I've cried like this and how Mum just hugged me until things didn't feel so bad, so I keep hugging Hetal as the rain keeps soaking us. After a few seconds, I feel her relax and she stops crying with a hiccup.

'Sorry about that,' she mutters. 'I don't know what's wrong with me.'

'We're all stressed,' I say. 'Let's ring the others, see if they've had any luck.'

I ring Cam, but they've not found Nell.

'Let's split up,' says Hetal. 'We'll cover a wider area, and if you find her, call me.'

I give Hetal a quick hug and we head in different directions. The path I go down is steep and has loose stones. I go carefully, my feet skidding and slipping from under me. My whole body's tense as I pick my way down, stopping to look around me and to call out for Nell.

At last. I'm near the bottom.

I jump down the last section. As I land, my foot twists, my ankle buckling with a sickening crump.

It's white-hot pain as I hop a couple of times before dropping to the ground.

I clutch my ankle and moan.

CHAPTER 26
HETAL

Saturday

I look down the path ahead of me and see Sasha, sitting, hunched on the ground. I pick my way down the path to her. She sounded awful on the phone. At first, I hadn't been able to understand what was wrong.

'Sasha! Are you okay?' I say as I reach her, crouching down beside her.

Sasha's clutching her ankle and groaning.

'What happened?' I ask.

'I twisted my ankle. It's so painful, I can't get up.'

She's shaking. Must be shock. I take off my raincoat and put it round her shoulders.

I check my phone. 'Nearest minor injuries clinic

isn't far away. If I help you, do you think you can stand?'

'How far is not far?'

'It's really close: 0.2 kilometres. Look, lean on me. You can do this.'

Sasha manages to stand, left leg off the ground, her arm around my shoulder. After we've gone a few steps it's obvious that 0.2 kilometres is going to feel like twenty at this rate.

'Let's take a break,' I say and Sasha wobbles and drops onto the grass beside the path.

I ring Cam. I'm pleased she decides to answer my call straight away this time and I quickly explain what's happened. We arrange for them to meet us at the bottom of the path.

Sasha's pale and shaking. Getting a lift is going to be our quickest option, but is it quick enough?

'Sasha? We've only got to get down these last few steps, then Cam will take us to the hospital. Do you think you can manage it?'

Sasha nods, her teeth gritted together as she stands back up again.

We inch down the steps, each one causing Sasha to suck in her breath.

Once we reach the road, we sit, waiting for Cam and Leo.

'I can't believe I'm so stupid,' says Sasha. 'We need to be out looking for Nell.'

I'm worried about Nell too. They say the first few hours when a person goes missing are the most important. The longer it is, the odds of finding her drop. But there's no way I'm sharing that with Sasha. She's got enough going on.

'I bet Nell's already back at the tent, reading our note and getting a bit annoyed that no one's come back yet.'

Sasha tries to smile, but it's clear I'm not fooling anyone.

A car tears up the road and screeches to a stop right by us. Cam almost falls out of the passenger side.

'You okay, Sash?' she asks.

'Never better,' says Sasha with a grimace.

'Let's get you to the hospital,' I say and we help Sasha into the car.

I direct Leo to the hospital which really isn't far at all. Leo drops us at the entrance, then goes to find a parking spot.

I check Sasha in and find out how long it'll take to be seen.

'They say it shouldn't be too long,' I say when I report back to Sasha and Cam.

Sasha's muttering to herself. Something about how's she going to manage high heels if she's twisted her ankle, and how she's going to ruin her dad's wedding day.

'Sasha? You okay?' I ask.

'Everything's gone wrong. We've lost Nell, and even if we find her when we get back to the tent, everything we have is soaked through, and even if we dry everything out, I won't be able to walk for the wedding tomorrow and that's if we even make it at all. It's like this whole trip wasn't meant to be.'

And I understand. I understand this on a molecular level. Every cell in my body is thinking the exact same thing. This trip was a mistake. We could have carried on pretending we were good friends if we hadn't gone on this trip. It used to be good, the best. But this last week has shown us how far we've grown apart.

I'm not even sure the others want to have our friendship back. Perhaps it's just me who's desperate for that. Everyone else seems to have moved on, found new people, got new directions in life. Perhaps I'm the only one that thinks our friendship is worth fighting for.

The nurse comes up to us with a wheelchair, helps Sasha into it and wheels her into the side room. Cam goes with her, followed by Leo who says he'll act as translator, even though I'm sure Sasha can manage.

And I'm left on my own, suddenly feeling very cold and very alone.

CHAPTER 27
NELL

Saturday

My feet are killing me. I have literally never walked so much in my entire life and I am exhausted. But it looks like the others are already back at the tent, because it's glowing from the inside and I can see shadows moving. As I get closer, I can hear everyone talking.

'When do we call the police?' Hetal says.

'How do I know?' Cam sounds angry. 'We don't even know why she left, or where she is. She might just be having a meltdown.'

Just having a meltdown? Is that what they think this is? I feel sick. This isn't what a meltdown is. Why doesn't Cam know that?

'That's a bit harsh,' says Sasha.

'She'll have overthought something and spiralled. She could have done with picking up her phone which is waiting for her in Marseille.'

'So that's my fault is it?' says Hetal.

I wish, for about the billionth time, that I had my own phone. I could have let them know I was lost, could have found my way back quicker. Maybe even been able to sort things out with Tom before it all imploded.

I bend and start to unzip the tent, when I'm deafened by screaming.

'It's Nell!'

'Nell? Is that you?'

'Where have you been? Honestly, you've been gone hours!'

I'm dragged into the tent and bombarded with questions and hugs.

'We've been so worried.'

'And in that storm too.'

'What happened? Why have you been gone so long?'

The only one not screaming at me is Leo who is sitting quietly, presumably waiting for the crazy shouting to stop.

'I'm fine,' I say. 'Got lost, wandered about a bit, sheltered from the storm in what turned out to be a pretty cool bar, lost track of time and came back. No biggie.' No meltdown, I want to say.

That stops them.

Three faces blankly stare back at me.

'No biggie?' says Hetal. 'You've been missing seven hours.'

'I wasn't missing,' I say. 'I knew where I was. Roughly. And I said I'd meet you back here.'

'We were out looking for you,' says Cam. 'Like for hours.'

'I'm sorry you were worried, okay? I didn't ask you to be.' I want to tell them about Tom and Ariel. I want to tell them how much that hurt. I want to say I'm sorry that I made them worried. But the meltdown comment overrides that. I don't want the sympathy or the special treatment.

I notice some crutches lying along the side of the tent.

'Whose are those?' I ask.

'Mine,' says Sasha. 'I twisted my ankle while we were out looking for you, so we've been to the hospital.'

Sasha got hurt looking for me? 'I'm sorry,' I mutter.

'Finally,' says Cam, 'an acknowledgement that you've caused some worry.'

'Wow, you sound just like my parents,' I snap back. What is with Cam at the moment? I grab some of my things.

'Where are you going now?'

'I'm going to have a shower. Turns out I need some space again.' And I push my way back out of the tent, grabbing my towel and wash bag as I go. I can't believe them. Anyone would think I'd pushed Sasha over on purpose. That this was all my fault.

I think of them all laughing at me falling in the fountain, of how funny they all thought it was. But I'm the one without a phone. No one really gets what it's been like without one. And today? Without a phone? Awful. The number of times I've gone to check something: a location, a time, a message, only to remember that I couldn't. And not being able to keep in easy contact with Tom has cost me that relationship.

I rage shower until I've washed all the anger away. I put on dry clothes and brush my hair and breathe and count in front of the mirror. I don't want to fall out with everyone, but then they're just so thoughtless. I'd taken myself off so my mood wouldn't ruin the whole day. But I guess I'd ruined it anyway.

I come out of the shower block and start

walking back to our tent. It's the wedding tomorrow. Perhaps when Sasha has done that, she'll be able to relax a bit more. I don't know what's going on with us. We used to be so close, but now we just snap at each other.

I feel a bit bad that Sasha's hurt herself while she was out looking for me. That's going to make tomorrow harder for her. I wonder if she's going to be okay to drive.

Across the field, in the darkness I can make out two figures standing by a car. Looks like it's Cam and Leo. Bet he's leaving.

Great, and now they're kissing. And I'm going to have to walk right past them to get to our tent. Ugh.

I mutter 'get a room' as I pass the car. They don't even notice I'm there.

It doesn't get any less awkward once I'm inside the tent. Hetal's busy making notes about something and Sasha's lying in her sleeping bag, scrolling on her phone. Neither of them says anything when I come in. So I get into bed and lie there, staring up at the little bugs swarming around the dangling torch.

How much of this trip do we have left? I don't even know. Too long. At least I'm picking up the phone Mum sent tomorrow.

The zip goes and Cam comes in. There's the sound of a car pulling away outside.

'Thanks for the support there, Nell,' says Cam. She's not smiling.

'What do you mean?' I ask.

'The "get a room" comment. You think I didn't hear?'

'What is it you always tell people? Just chill out?' I say. 'Not so easy to chill out when it's you, is it?'

Cam doesn't say anything else, and I just turn over and pretend to go to sleep.

Hetal coughs. 'Just to remind everyone it's the wedding tomorrow. So we have to be off early, all packed up, no excuses, okay?'

I mutter 'okay' and Cam does too.

Great. Everyone is absolutely in the right mood for a party. What could go wrong?

CHAPTER 28
CAM

Sunday – Wedding Day

Madge is licking my face. Clearly she thinks I'm lacking in personal hygiene and need a thorough clean.

'Stop that,' I whisper, gently pushing her away and trying not to wake the others. But she's not put off, coming back to lick my ear. I take the hint and head over to the shower block with Madge on her lead. She's delighted to be out, pouncing on flies and insects on the way. I fix her lead at the end of the shower, outside the shower curtain and turn on the water. I let the water run over me.

My mind is churning this morning. It's a battle between the happy glow after yesterday with Leo and the texts he's been sending since, and playing what my grandmother said over and over in my head. The toxic wins. *Your sort, your sort.* I phrase and rephrase what I should have said in reply. Then Phil's words join in. *It was a bad idea, taking you to see my parents.* A bad idea. That's me.

I get out of the shower and scrub myself dry with a towel, rage pulsing through my veins. I've tried to ignore it, tried to ignore what happened, forget how much it hurt but I can't. It's there, all the time, burning into my brain, making me think they might have a point. That there's something wrong with me.

I get dressed and sit on the grass. Madge climbs onto my lap and nudges my hand until I'm forced to tickle her ears. She seems to like me, just accepts me for who I am, loves me regardless. I sigh. Perhaps that's what I can't ignore. Why I can't answer Phil's calls. I'm hiding from the future. The future where I don't have a family I can rely on. I'd dropped my defences, allowed myself to believe Phil would be there even when I'd outgrown foster care, when I was officially 'grown-up'. I can't carry on like this. Ignoring the problem just isn't working, it's eating away at me, and I can't even enjoy meeting a guy like Leo without this whole thing souring it. I wish it wouldn't, but wishing isn't working.

Besides, since when have I hidden from my problems? If Phil has regrets about me, about who I am then I want to hear them. I can't live in this limbo anymore, wondering if I can still see Maisie and Erin. I never thought he had a problem with me before, so what's changed? Has what happened at his parents' house changed how he sees me?

I find my phone and call him, before I have time to think, before I have time to chicken out.

'Hello? Cam? Is everything okay?'

He sounds worried.

'Hi, no, everything's fine.' Only it isn't. 'I need to talk to you, about what happened.'

'Of course.'

'You said it was a bad idea to take me to see your parents. I don't get why.'

'Do you think it went well?' He sounds surprised.

'No! Of course not. It was a total train wreck.'

He chuckles. Why is he laughing?

'Firstly Cam, I need to apologise. It was all my fault.'

'It's not your fault your mum's a total…' I search for the right, least offensive word.

'I didn't exactly give her the best chance.'

'What do you mean?'

'I hadn't told her about you. Not until the day before we went to stay.'

I'm holding the phone and I'm hearing the words but it feels like a dream. A nightmare. He hadn't told his own mother about me? 'Why not?' I whisper.

'It was a stupid decision. I didn't think it through. I was wrong. So very, very wrong. I should have told her when I first found you. But I didn't. I think I was worried it wouldn't work out and then she'd never let me live it down. I'm her only child. In her eyes I'm perfect or, at least, I have to give the impression I am.'

I can't speak. My own dad is embarrassed of me?

'But you have turned out to be one of the best things ever to happen to me. You have no idea what an amazing young person you are. And I'm so proud and privileged to be your father. And I know I can't take credit for you. You've turned out like this in spite of me not because of me. And now I've gone and messed it all up.' He pauses. 'I should have told them about you sooner; I should have stood by you when we got to their house; I should have insisted you were treated fairly. That you got a fair shot. And I let you down. My mum and dad have no idea how amazing you are because they didn't give you a chance, and I didn't encourage them to.'

I don't know what to say. I suppose it does at least explain why his mum was so hostile. It's quite a big thing to wrap your brain around, an extra granddaughter.

'Cam? You still there?'

'Yeah.'

'I'm sorry. I've messed up big time.'

I think of all the times I've spent round at their house, all the times chatting to him over tea, all the fun with Maisie and Erin, all the time I've felt like I've belonged.

'Well, we all mess up sometimes,' I say.

'This is literally my biggest ever.'

'What do we do about your parents?'

He sighs. 'I've talked to them a lot over the last few days. It might take them some time.'

'Be honest. Have they changed their opinion of me at all?'

He pauses. 'No. And that's their loss.'

It is true then. My grandparents don't want anything to do with me.

I pause, wondering if I've got the courage to ask the question that's been burning in my brain.

'Does this change anything between us?' It's almost a whisper. Please. Please don't say this is it. That he chooses them over me. That he's going to cut me loose from his family. That I'll have to have a future alone, without them. I don't think I could take that.

'What?'

Is he angry?

'Can I still see you, see Maisie and Erin?' Can I still be in your family?

'Cam! Of course. This has no effect on our relationship. What. So. Ever. Actually, ignore that, it does make a difference. I am determined to be there for you. At every point you need me, at every step in your life. I want to be a proper dad. Someone you can count on every time.'

I can't speak for a moment.

'Thanks for telling me everything, Phil. It helps. I didn't have a clue what I'd done wrong, and I couldn't understand why they acted like that.'

'You did nothing wrong. I should have warned you.'

'Yeah, you should've,' I say.

'Anytime you need to talk, I'm here for you. I'm never going to let you down like that again. I promise.'

'And what about Maisie and Erin?'

'Are you kidding? They love you to the moon and back. They were worried you'd left, but I explained you had to go. They can't wait to see you when you get back.'

After I hang up, Madge runs around me, getting her lead wrapped round my legs, as I try and get my head around what Phil said. I pick her up and hold her close. Everyone says finding your birth family can be a rocky process and, until now, it has gone so well. It would be naïve to think it would all be smooth and straightforward.

Trusting a new dad has taken time. And I guess, trusting a new daughter might take time too. I tickle Madge's ears and she licks my nose. If only it could all be as simple as her. I wonder if Madge is missing her family. I hold her tight and think how hard it's going to be to hand her back to the campsite when we go home.

I smile and walk slowly back to the tent.

'Cam! There you are. Where the hell have you been? We should have left ages ago.'

Hetal's stressed and Sasha looks furious.

Oh crap. The wedding.

CHAPTER 29
SASHA

Sunday – Wedding Day

This is just like Cam. So wrapped up in her own stuff she forgets everyone else. My ankle is aching, and my brain is wired. It's the wedding day and I could do without Cam trying to ruin it.

I'm wearing the best outfit I own; an off-the-shoulder jumpsuit. Every time I wear it, I always get the best comments. I slip my feet into my heels. Now to see if I can stand.

'Agh, that's not good,' I say, my left foot throbbing as I try and balance on it.

'Perhaps heels are going to be a step too far,' says Nell.

'But this outfit needs heels.'

Hetal eyes up my shoes. 'Well, you can either choose to wear heels, or you can choose to walk.'

'Ha, very funny,' I say. I put my trainers on, thinking I'll change later. No point in having the pain all the way there.

We finish off packing the car now Cam's here. Everyone's on edge and snapping at each other. Cam scoops up Madge and we finally leave. I check the time. It's going to be really tight. I wince as I accelerate. I brake and the pain is worse.

'Is it your ankle?' asks Hetal. 'Perhaps you shouldn't be driving.'

'And miss my dad's wedding? After everything? Not a chance.'

'In which case, just take it really steady.'

As if I have any choice. With my ankle throbbing with every movement, we take the road out along the coast. The sea glitters in the early morning sunshine. Everything feels fresher and cooler after yesterday's storm as we pick our way along the road, windows down and music up.

'Where did you say the wedding venue is?' asks Hetal, looking down at her phone.

'*La Maison de la Falaise*,' I say. 'It means Clifftop House.'

'That sounds gorgeous,' says Nell. I see her in

the rear-view mirror, staring out to sea. She hasn't asked to borrow my phone in a while. I wonder what's going on with her and Tom, though I'm not going to ask until later. Can't deal with the drama today.

'I think Dad wants to give Clarisse a really special day,' I say. 'So I guess the venue will be beautiful.'

Thankfully, there's no traffic, and we screech into the car park of *La Maison de la Falaise* with two minutes to spare. I abandon the car diagonally in a parking space and try and wrestle my crutches out of the car. I'm late, and hobbling. There's no way I'm going to make a quiet entrance. I'm going to do exactly what I didn't want to do; ruin everything.

I leave the others with the keys and limp over to the hotel. I was expecting more people to be here if I'm honest. The place feels deserted. I go into the reception and ask about the wedding.

The receptionist looks puzzled. Did I say something wrong in French?

'*Desole, il n'y a pas de marriage ici aujourd'hui.*'

I must have misheard. Or misunderstood.

I check but the answer is the same. There is no wedding here today.

I turn and hurry back out to the car, my ankle

screaming in pain. The others are still gathered around the car.

'Sasha? You okay?' calls Hetal.

'They say there isn't a wedding here today.'

'What?' Hetal looks horrified. 'Quick, find the invitation on your phone. We need to check the date.'

My hands are shaking as I find the email. I check. The date is correct. It's today. And the time. And then I spot it. The venue is *L'Auberge de la Falaise* – Clifftop Inn, not Clifftop House.

Hetal's ahead of me and is finding out directions. She looks up, her face already telling me it's not good.

'It's the other side of town. If we're quick, we might get there in half an hour. In time for the reception maybe…'

Her voice trails off.

I sit down on the floor, all the energy leaking out of me. I don't know why I even thought this was a good idea. All I wanted to do was not mess this up.

And I would have done if it wasn't for my friends.

'Well, thanks a lot, everyone,' I say. 'All I wanted to do was get to my father's wedding. It's not like it was *the entire point* of our trip or anything. You were all supposed to be here for support. But no. You guys had to go and mess it all up. Thanks, Cam, for making us late. Thanks, Nell, for going missing yesterday, which caused my injury and meant we had to drive here at the pace of a snail making us even later. And thanks, Hetal, for not bothering to check the venue beforehand. Seriously. Thanks for nothing.'

There's not a sound except the sea birds circling us, calling to each other.

Hetal's the first to speak. 'I'm so sorry, Sasha. You're right. I should have checked.'

Cam cuts in. 'Don't be ridiculous. Sasha gave you the wrong details. You shouldn't have to apologise.'

What the actual…?

Before I have a chance to say anything, Cam carries on. 'But I definitely owe you an apology. It is totally my fault we were late this morning. I could have called home later on. I knew what was happening today, and I should have realised how important it was.'

'I'm sorry too,' says Nell, her voice wobbling a bit. 'I had no idea you'd all be out looking for me.'

I look at them all. I know they mean it. But that

doesn't stop the disappointment of missing my dad's wedding.

'Hate to break this moment up with practicalities,' says Hetal. 'And I know you all hate me for organising you. But I think it's still worth setting off to the wedding. We can talk later. For now, we have a wedding to get to.'

The next hour is a blur of traffic, blaring horns and busy streets. But all I can hear is my dad's voice. *Unreliable. Bad attitude.*

I swerve into the car park and abandon my car at the end of a row of cars. We're definitely in the right place this time. It's packed with people.

I leave the others and hobble in, only realising once I'm inside that I still have my trainers on. I haven't got time to change them. I half hop, half run across the lobby towards the room where the vows are being said.

'Sasha! *Ma belle*!'

It's Clarisse. She's stood at the bottom of the wide, curving stairs, looking stunning in a long, white dress.

'You… I… You look amazing,' I say, going over to her.

'You're limping?' Her face creases as she looks down at my feet.

'Yes. Long story. And I was supposed to have better shoes on. But I went to the wrong venue, and now I'm late, and I'm messing it all up. Which was the last thing I wanted to do...' I trail off. She doesn't want to hear all that.

'I know. Hetal's been in touch. We've delayed the start for you. Though I've not told your dad. It'll be a surprise, no?' She's beaming.

'You've waited for me?' And Hetal sorted it out?

She whispers something to the man with her, who I presume is her father. He nods, kisses her cheek, smiles at me and walks away to the car park.

'Now,' Clarisse says, 'come with me.'

'But?' I say. 'Aren't you supposed to be getting married? I don't want to make you any later.'

'Your father can wait.'

I follow her up the stairs to her hotel room. She unlocks the door and I go in after her. It's a luxurious suite, with an enormous bed and views out over the sea.

Hung on the outside of the wardrobe is the bridesmaid's dress.

'I brought it. Just in case you came,' she explains.

'Where are your other bridesmaids?'

'I only ever had one. You.'

I blink. I was her only bridesmaid? I'd assumed I was the 'duty' bridesmaid. The one she had to ask.

'Sasha?'

I don't know what to say. All the thoughts about Clarisse being the one who encouraged Dad to get back in touch come crowding into my brain.

'It's okay if you don't want to be my bridesmaid. There's no pressure. I'm just so pleased you came.'

'Last summer,' I say, 'was it your idea to invite me to Geneva?'

She nods.

I think of the trips I've made to see Dad and Clarisse over the last year. Each time it was an email from Clarisse inviting me. She's the one helping my dad to find a way to make our relationship work. She's the glue holding us together.

'I would love to be your bridesmaid,' I say shakily. I can't believe she brought the dress. That she only chose me.

She claps her hands excitedly. 'Then we must be quick!'

I change in the bathroom. Luckily the dress is long enough to cover my trainers. Before I go out, I look in the mirror. The dress is still the ugliest dress I've ever seen, but for some reason that doesn't matter so much anymore. It's what it stands for that counts. It's a physical sign that Clarisse wants me here.

'Oh, you look lovely,' Clarisse exclaims as I walk out of the bathroom. She tweaks my hair into shape and fixes a flower behind my ear. 'Perfect.'

We walk together down the stairs. Her dad's waiting by the closed double doors and inside we can hear the string quartet playing and the gentle chatter of the guests. The usher smiles at us, makes the signal to the musicians and, as they finish their piece, pushes the doors open wide.

The room is grand, with a high ceiling and lined with rows of seats, all filled with smartly dressed guests. I am to walk down the aisle ahead of Clarisse and her father. I take a deep breath, ready to start walking when the music starts again. Then I spot them.

Nell and Cam. Dressed up and looking amazing, sitting on the back row! But where's Hetal? I don't have time to wonder, as I'm walking past them and down the aisle.

Despite my ankle, I feel like I'm gliding, everyone's smiling and nodding at me as I pass them. My dad turns, expecting only to see Clarisse. Then he sees me.

In that moment, every doubt I ever had about

being here evaporates. By the time I get to the front, he has tears rolling down his cheeks. He reaches out to me and gives me the biggest hug. And as Clarisse arrives behind us, she gets pulled in too.

My dad's getting married, and I'm so pleased I'm here. And in every possible way, he's telling me he's happy I'm here too.

CHAPTER 30
HETAL

Sunday

Clarisse's dad asked us into the wedding and Cam and Nell have gone in. But I can't. The adrenaline of getting here and desperately trying to get everything to work out has gone and now I feel empty. Like I've got nothing left. Like I want to sit down and never move again.

I get out my phone and call Nani. When she picks up, I can hear music in the background, with laughter and shouting.

'Nani?'

'Ah, Hetal, my precious. How's the road trip going?'

'Not great.' I hear movements and the music

and laughter get quieter.

'Not great? Are you okay? Is anyone hurt?'

Only my pride I want to say. 'No, we're all fine. It's just that some plans haven't worked out. And I'm worried it's ruined the whole holiday.'

'Oh, my love. You won't have ruined anything.'

'I have. We stayed in a campsite full of cows.'

'So?'

'What do you mean, so? There were cows. They scared us half to death in the middle of the night.'

Nani laughs. 'That sounds just like a trip I went on when I was younger. Only it was sheep. My friends and I have been laughing about that night for fifty years.'

'Laughing about it? But didn't it ruin your camping trip?'

'Well, it ruined the tent. They chewed a dirty great big hole in the corner of it. We had to stuff it with our bags to keep the rain out.' She chuckles again. 'Best camping trip ever.'

'Bet you never bought fake festival tickets though.'

'Does being totally conned by a time-share scam in my thirties count?'

'In your thirties?'

'Yes! These con artists are very clever. Good at picking up on your weak spots.'

I think back to the stall where I bought the tickets. The man had asked about my friends and said what a brilliant way it would be to surprise everyone with tickets. He certainly knew my weak spot.

'Listen, Hetal, everyone makes mistakes. Everyone. But it's what you do with those mistakes that counts. You can either give up or learn from them and try again.'

'And I think our friendship is over. It's all weird, and everyone's saying mean stuff. And I thought I was going to be friends with them forever.'

Nani pauses. 'Friendships are funny things. Some friends come and go. Friends for a season, the friendship blooms and fades, and that's okay. It happens to everyone. It's hard letting go because the friendship was so beautiful.'

I feel a sob bubbling up. 'I don't want it to be over though.'

'I know. But there is another type of friendship. One which weathers the storm. You have your ups and downs, like all friendships do, but you fight for it. You fight for your friendship. You work at it. You have those tough conversations. You share your feelings honestly and when life hits you hard, they are there for you, no matter what.'

'But how do you know which friendship it is?'

'Oh, that's easy. Do you want to fight for it, or do you want to walk away?'

Nani's right.

'Thanks, Nani. And sorry for disturbing your holiday. How is Kent by the way?'

'Absolutely brilliant! I'm next up for the dance-off competition.'

I laugh. 'In which case, good luck! Go show them how it's done.'

After I hang up, I think about what she said. About mistakes. And what you do with them. About friendships and how you can repair them. I'll start fighting for my friendships right after the wedding. But there's someone else. Someone else who I've not fought for.

I chew my lip as I start texting.

Finn, I should have said this sooner. I'm sorry. I messed it all up and I should have realised. I was so busy with schoolwork that I forgot to talk to you. And I reassured myself that I'd make it up to you in the summer. That I'd plan to see you in the holidays and it would make up for everything. It doesn't and I'm sorry. If I could do it all over again, I'd do it differently. I'd send you animal gifs back; I'd call you just before I went to sleep; I'd make space for you in my life. I made a mistake. I don't expect anything, just wanted to say I get why you ended things. It was the right thing to do.

I read it through, then press send.

I sneak into the back of the wedding room. Sasha looks so happy! Nell and Cam move up so I can sit next to them. The service is in French, but I'm managing to pick up the general gist. The officiator is talking and now he's asking for something. He's looking from Clarisse to Sasha's dad, then to the best man.

'What the heck is going on? Are you understanding any of this?' whispers Cam in my ear.

'No! Not a clue.'

A woman in front turns round and smiles, then gently tells us in English that the ring has been forgotten.

What? Oh no! The whole thing's ruined. The best man whispers to Sasha's dad. Then stands up and says something to the guests. There's some shuffling and whispering, then a couple of people stand up, taking off rings as they walk to the front.

'He's asked if there are any rings he can borrow,' whispers the woman in front.

I'm dying of cringe inside. If only the best man had thought it through, if only he'd remembered to put the rings in his pocket. I feel so painfully awkward for him.

But he doesn't look phased at all. He kisses the ring-owners, takes their rings and hands them to the officiator.

Sasha's dad's smiling and Clarisse is too and when they come to say their vows and put the rings on, they both smile towards the people who offered their rings. It's a lovely moment. How did that happen? Something like that could have ruined the whole ceremony but it hasn't. It might even be that it made it better. The woman in front says the officiator is talking about being connected, not only to each other, but to everyone in this room who are witnesses and are part of the community who will support their marriage, and in very practical ways. Everyone laughs.

I start to relax. There's nothing I need to organise today. Everything about this day has been thought through and prepared. If something goes wrong, it gets sorted. I don't know what the timings are so I can't worry if it's running behind schedule and in fact, as a guest, I'm not expected even to help with anything. The feeling is weird. For weeks, probably months, I've been carrying an expectation. That I'll always plan the day, work out the most efficient use of my time and achieve my best in everything I do.

It's exhausting.

No one here looks exhausted with the organisation. I'm guessing Clarisse has done a lot of it, but she doesn't look stressed, doesn't have a to-do list tucked in her bouquet, isn't checking the clock to see if they're on time.

How does she manage it? I watch her through the service. Everyone has their job to do. Admittedly the best man failed to bring the rings, but he sorted it out. He found a way to make it work. Clarisse didn't feel the need to jump in and take over.

What if that's the way to make it work? By sharing it out.

Could I do that?

I organised everything about this trip, even though I wasn't supposed to be coming on it. Was that a good thing to do? I thought I was helping, and Sasha did seem grateful, but was I really forcing them to do what *I* wanted to do? And Cam had said that she wished there was more adventurous stuff and I hadn't even thought about that!

I chew my bottom lip as the service finishes and

the couple sweep back up the aisle, followed by Sasha. She gives us a tiny wave on her way past.

I feel my phone ping, so I check it. A text from Finn. I click on it, fingers trembling.

How about we meet up later in the summer, and see how things go?

I stare at the words, all the letters dancing in front of my eyes.

I would love to.

Let's chat when you get back from France.

I smile. He knows I'm in France which means he's been checking out my socials. There still might be hope.

By the time we get out of the ceremony room, the photographs are underway. Clarisse has asked us all to stay for the day. Nell has collected her new phone and goes to sit on a bench overlooking the gardens. Cam and I get drinks and sit on the terrace watching the other guests chat and mingle.

'I'm really glad we made it,' says Cam, as she sips her drink. 'Sasha looks so pleased to be here.'

'She does,' I say, looking over at Sasha whose face is lit up chatting to her dad.

Cam looks sideways at me. 'And are you okay? I feel like we might not be in a great place, me and you.'

I know what she means. 'I don't think we are. But I reckon we can fix it. If you want to give it a try?' I hold my breath, hoping with all my heart that she wants to fight for our friendship too.

'I'd like that,' she says. 'Maybe we've both had a lot going on?'

I certainly feel that way. And if Cam is feeling like that too, then no wonder we'd snapped at each other.

'I think everything got on top of me. You know sometimes everything you do goes wrong, and I felt like that. I'd tried my best and it still hadn't worked out.'

Cam frowns. 'What do you mean? Everything you do is brilliant. You are amazing at school, and the way you've organised this road trip? It's been mind-blowing.'

I shake my head. 'The barbeque though, the terrible campsite, then checking where the wedding was today. I've let everyone down so much.'

Cam turns to me. 'Rubbish. You never let people down. Remember last night? You knew exactly where the hospital was. You knew exactly what to do. I mean, you were the only one who had planned for emergencies. We'd have been lost without you.'

'Yes, but the cows!'

Cam laughs. 'You weren't to know there were going to be escaped cows.'

'I should have realised we hadn't been booked into that campsite.'

'Who checks their spam? Honestly, Hetal, you are awesome. You're way too hard on yourself.'

I nod. I daren't speak as tears are threatening. 'There's no excuse for the festival tickets though.' I finally manage. 'I really am so sorry.'

Cam puts her arm around me. 'You don't have to be perfect for people to love you, you know. And this trip doesn't have to run like clockwork for us to have a good time. Not that we don't appreciate you trying,' she says, grinning. 'But every now and again, it's okay to get it wrong. It's okay to cut yourself some slack. It's your holiday too.'

Sasha comes up to us, her face lit up with excitement. 'Isn't this brilliant? Are you both okay? Where's Nell?'

Cam nods in the direction of Nell, who is head down, tapping on her phone.

'You all look so good. I'd no idea you guys had brought such gorgeous clothes with you!'

We laugh. 'There was the outside chance we might be going to a wedding,' I say.

'Mine's all down to Hetal,' says Cam. 'She has

next level organisational skills and picked it up when she collected my passport.'

Cam's smiling at me, and it feels good. Good to be getting back to us.

'Speaking of which,' Cam continues, 'are we loving the dress?' She's eyeing up Sasha's bridesmaid's dress.

'Absolutely not,' Sasha says, hobbling a spin round. 'It is just as hideous as I remember, but it's weird… Somehow it doesn't matter. Something I *never* thought I'd say.'

'Hang on, have you got *trainers* on?' says Cam.

Sasha lifts up her dress to show us. 'Clarisse said I could, which is handy 'cause I couldn't walk in anything else. That's one good thing about this dress I suppose!'

Cam laughs.

'And is everything okay with your dad?' I ask, reckoning I already know the answer.

'Yes!' Sasha's smiling more than I've seen her smiling in weeks. 'Thanks so much for getting me here, Hetal. And for messaging Clarisse to make sure they waited. That was top-tier friendship love right there.'

CHAPTER 31
NELL

Sunday

Sasha's talking to Cam and Hetal. I can hear their laughter above all the chatter of the other guests. It helps to know they're happy. I can't seem to find that happiness in me though. I've set the new phone up. I feel the panic of not being connected start to subside and my shoulders drop. I can't bring myself to look though. I haven't checked since I sent that Instagram message to Tom. I told myself I wouldn't. It's over. I can't believe he did this. How could he? I've only been gone a week and he's already back with Ariel.

I look over the garden which gently slopes before dropping off to the sea. This place is gorgeous. It feels like a place I should be happy but I can't shake the empty feeling inside me. I didn't fool myself that I'd be with Tom forever, that's not it. It's just it didn't feel like we'd be over so soon.

I suppose I can't put it off anymore. I click open my phone and go to my Instagram account.

There's the message I sent.

I can't believe what you've done. It's over. We're over. I'm done.

Underneath that there is message after message after message.

What have I done?
Nell?
What do you mean we're over?
You must have given Sasha her phone back.
Call me. Please Nell. As soon as you get this.
It can't be over.
Please Nell, can we talk?
Whatever it is I've done, I'm sorry.

I frown. Does he really not know why I'm upset? I would have thought it's obvious.

Nell! You're online. I can see you are. Please. I'm going to call you. Please answer.

Dammit. I can't even sneak online without everyone knowing.

The phone vibrates and I answer.

'Hello?'

Tom's worried face appears on the screen. 'Hi, Nell! I'm so glad you answered. I've been logged on waiting to see if you would for hours.'

He has?

'Whatever I've done, I'm sorry. Just don't finish with me. Not without telling me what's wrong.'

'You don't know?'

'No idea. Not a clue. But whatever it is, I never meant to hurt you. I never meant to upset you. Please, Nell.'

My hands are shaking. I didn't really want to have this conversation but here we go. 'I saw Ariel's Instagram. About you and her. Did you think if I wasn't around, I wouldn't know?'

'Ariel? What's she got to do with this?'

'Everything. Obviously.'

'Hang on.' He clicks on his screen, and I watch as his face concentrates, scrolling through posts, then stops, reads and his face drops.

'Nell! I have no idea what she's on about, but it's not what you're thinking. Ariel and I are over, we have been for ages. She's working at the deli, but that's it. I haven't seen her other than that. I had no idea she'd been posting that stuff. I only commented on the first one because she tagged me in. I thought I was being friendly. But I swear. That was it.'

Do I believe him? I look at him, his face creased with worry. He could be lying. Or he could be telling the truth.

'Who was with you on the beach the other night when I rang?'

'On the beach? That was Isaac. He was being daft and I was trying to tell him to stop.'

So it hadn't been Ariel.

'What about that last photo? Of you kissing Ariel?' I almost choke on the words as I say them.

'Taken last summer. Look at my ear in the photo. It's not pierced. Which dates it pre-Christmas.' He's smiling.

I smile back.

'You really thought I'd cheat on you?'

'I dunno. Maybe? I'm not around, and we've not being going out all that long. And then Ariel working at the deli…'

'Well, you know I can't resist anyone who smells like sausage rolls,' he says, teasing.

I laugh. I can't help it. 'I guess I was worried you wouldn't want to stay with me.'

'Want to know something?'

'Okay?'

'I've been thinking the exact same thing.'
What?
'I've been imagining you road tripping around France, different town every couple of days. You'll be meeting loads of people, loads of amazing French people, all speaking the language of lurve. And what does boring old Tom, the nephew of a deli-owner, have on them? You'd dump me for sure. And then you did.'

He'd been worried about me? I can't help myself. I start laughing and can't stop.

'You thought I…' I gasp for breath, '…would cheat on you? That's crazy. I never would! How about, in the future, I'll try and talk to you first, rather than letting my worry run away with me.'

Tom smiles. 'I know we haven't been together all that long but, honestly, I've never felt like this about anyone before. I promise I'll try hard to be honest. And I absolutely promise to never, ever, two-time you.'

In an instant, my world feels brighter, like there are possibilities and I'm back to grinning like my face might split.

'I really wish I wasn't in France right now.'

'I really wish you weren't either. Where are you by the way? It looks a bit posh.'

I pan the camera round and Tom whistles.

'We're at Sasha's dad's wedding. Long story short, we've scored a day of free food and sea views.'

'Nice. I hope you have an amazing day.'

I notice the time. 'Aren't you supposed to be in work?' It's a Sunday, Wendy will need him there.

'I rang in to say I had to try and get in contact with you. Aunt Wendy understood. Suppose I had better go and help out now though.'

'Okay. See you in a week.'

'Can't wait.'

I put the phone in my pocket, lean back on the bench and look out to sea. It really is a beautiful place. And this time I feel the happiness tingle through me.

'Nell!' There's a shout from behind me. It's Hetal, Cam and Sasha. A band has started playing and they're the first up on the outdoor dance floor.

I go over and get pulled into the circle, and I laugh and dance and lose myself in the music.

CHAPTER 32
CAM

Sunday

It's nearly midnight, the band are still playing but we're all danced out: well, Sasha's foot started really aching, so we all decided to take a break and now we're lying out on the lawns, heads together, looking up at the stars.

'Did you know you can see Jupiter?' says Hetal.

'Where is it?' asks Nell.

'I love that you know where Jupiter is,' I say. 'I mean, I have a rough idea. It's in space. But I can't get any more specific.'

Everyone laughs.

'Thanks for being here today,' says Sasha. 'I was so sure I was going to mess everything up, but it's been the exact opposite. Thank you so much for convincing me. And I'm sorry I lost my cool when we went to the wrong place. There was no excuse.'

'I'm sorry I added to your stress,' I say. 'You told us how important it was to you, and I should have listened.'

'I'm sorry I've been a bit of a downer all week,' says Nell. She seems happier this evening.

'Everything okay?' asks Hetal.

'Yeah. Sorted everything out with Tom. We're all good.'

I can hear her smiling in the darkness and it makes me happy too. Funny how we're still so connected.

'I've learnt something this week,' says Hetal. 'I've realised that sometimes you can plan and plan something and it doesn't work out. And other times, you can have the best day ever, and you didn't plan a thing.'

Sasha agrees. 'That's so true.'

'I think you underestimate how many good things you make happen, Hetal,' I say.

'What, like the cows?' she says, laughing.

We all laugh.

'I was so scared,' says Sasha, laughing. 'And Nell

was out there, when we thought someone was creeping around in the dark.'

We laugh again.

'Has it been stressing you out?' Sasha asks Hetal.

'Yeah, a bit. It doesn't usually, but it's been a full-on few months, and I've been working so hard, and I don't seem to be able to do anything right. And I've realised I wasn't sharing any of this with you guys, because I didn't want to ruin our friendship with all of the stuff that's been going on. But perhaps I need to share. Perhaps that's what makes our friendship stronger.'

'Makes sense,' I say. Should I tell them about my grandparents? Would I be ruining this moment by sharing that? I thought I was doing the right thing by keeping it to myself.

'Sounds like you need a holiday,' says Nell.

'Well, I do have a suggestion,' says Hetal.

'Let's hear it,' I say.

'How about we all take a day each on the way home, we each decide what we're going to do that day, where we're going to go and what we're going to eat. And that way, everyone gets to do something they enjoy, with us all, and I get some time where I don't have to think or worry or plan. What do you think?'

'That sounds like a good idea!' says Sasha.

'Brace yourselves for an adrenaline-fuelled day,' I say, laughing. Or maybe, just maybe, if I'm extra brave, I'll suggest we go home via Brive-la-Gaillarde and Leo.

We're all quiet for a moment, looking up at the stars. The more you look, the more there are, as each little twinkle of light turns out to be thousands of tiny lights sparkling together. A star shoots across the sky.

'Did you see it?' says Hetal.

'Yes! A shooting star!' says Nell.

'Aren't you supposed to make a wish?' says Sasha.

'You don't believe that, do you?' I say.

'What's the downside?' says Hetal. 'It's like visualisation – if you wish for something hard enough it can happen.'

I think about my grandparents. Do I wish that they would love me? It doesn't feel quite right somehow. No. I wish that I'm happy regardless of what they think of me. I smile up at the stars and wish it with all my heart.

'So, my grandparents…' I say. Instantly everyone is silent, listening. 'Turns out they're not so lovely.'

'Oh, Cam. I'm so sorry,' says Nell. 'Are you okay?'

'I am. Phil hadn't told them about me until the day before we went, so I think I came as a bit of a surprise.'

'That's really odd,' says Sasha. 'What did your grandparents do?'

I tell them about them ignoring me, planning a daytrip without me and taking the pink felt tip out of the packet.

Sasha swears. 'Wow, that is messed up. You're better off without that sort of toxicity in your life.'

'You really are,' says Nell. 'And like I said before, it's their loss. They have no idea what a wonderful person they're missing out on.'

'Want to know the really messed up part? I felt like I couldn't trust anyone anymore. Even you guys. I'm so sorry for being short-tempered all week. I was so wrapped up with what happened and with what Phil had said that I couldn't see how I was snapping at everyone all the time. I don't want to be a friend like that.'

I feel Nell squeeze my hand and Hetal says, 'Don't be daft. We get it.'

'Yeah, we get it,' says Sasha. 'But tell us next time, okay? We're here for you.'

'Always,' says Nell.

A tear slides down the side of my face.

'I've figured out that there's no such thing as a perfect family,' I say. 'Everyone's got their thing.'

'Nothing's perfect,' says Hetal. 'Even if I really try!'

'Not family, not boyfriends, not friends, not life,' says Sasha.

'Hey, boyfriends aren't all bad,' says Nell, making us all laugh.

'Cats are pretty cool too,' I say tickling Madge's ears. I can't leave her behind. First thing tomorrow I'm going to ring the campsite and see if I can keep her.

'But some friends can be pretty damn awesome,' Sasha says. 'Thanks for sticking with me today.'

'It's what friends do,' says Nell.

'Want to know what I wished for?' says Hetal. 'I wished we'd still be together in fifty years, laughing like this and remembering the good times, sharing our problems and sticking by each other no matter what.'

Another star shoots across the sky and I can almost hear everyone wishing the same thing. Here's to another fifty summers with the best friends in the whole wide world.

ACKNOWLEDGEMENTS

Firstly, my deep and heartfelt thanks to my agent, Hannah Sheppard, for being an incredible human being. Thank you for continuing to believe in me even when I didn't. Thank you for being kind when things were tough. And thank you for being thoughtful, considered and bang on with your editorial comments.

Thanks to the amazing Firefly Press. To Janet Thomas and Hayley Fairhead, my editors, who have given such brilliant edits and insights. Thank you for your tireless passion for this story. To Amy Low for an awesome cover. And to the whole Firefly Team for all the energy you put in. Thanks for sticking by me.

Thanks to those who introduce teenagers to my stories: librarians, booksellers, teachers, bloggers, parents. Your enthusiasm is infectious, and it means the world to me.

Thank you to my friends, family and fellow writers for listening, offering advice or a shoulder, for buying, for your interest and excitement. It would be a lonelier, lesser life without you.

To Mark, Sophie, Rory, Noah and Tilda – I love you.

And to you, my reader. Thank you for trusting me with your time.

ABOUT THE AUTHOR

Kate Mallinder lives with her family near Ashby-de-la-Zouch in Leicestershire. She grew up in Solihull and lived for a while in West Yorkshire. She is fascinated by what makes people tick and writing is her way of exploring that. Even after writing *Summer of No Regrets*, Sasha, Hetal, Nell and Cam still had more to say, so she followed them on a road trip. *Summer Under the Stars* is her third novel.

Do you want to find out how Sasha, Hetal, Nell and Cam spent last summer? Be sure to read *Summer of No Regrets*, out now!

Praise for *Summer of No Regrets*

'A wonderful summer, happy-ending story about friendship. I raced through it.'
Perdita Cargill

'…a complete page turner.'
Jenny McLachlan

'It was such a fun and easy read and is absolutely perfect for the summer!'
A. M. Dassu

At Firefly we care very much about the environment and our responsibility to it. Many of our stories involve the natural world, our place in it and what we can all do to help it, and us, survive the challenges of the climate emergency. Go to our website www.fireflypress.co.uk to find more of our great stories that focus on the environment, like **Aubrey and the Terrible Ladybirds**, **The Song that Sings Us** and **My Name is River**.

As a Wales-based publisher we are also very proud of the beautiful natural places, plants and animals in our country on the western side of Great Britain.

We are always looking at reducing our impact on the environment, including our carbon footprint and the materials we use, and are taking part in UK-wide publishing initiatives to improve this wherever we can.